This 1992 edition published by Dorset Press,
a division of Marboro Books Corporation,
by arrangement with Grisewood & Dempsey Ltd.

ISBN 0–88029–741–7

Printed in United States

10 9 8 7 6 5 4 3 2 1

ACKNOWLEDGMENTS

The Publishers gratefully acknowledge permission to reproduce
the following copyright material:

Margaret Mahy: for *Don't Cut the Lawn!* from "The Downhill Crocodile Whizz
and Other Stories," reprinted by permission of J M Dent & Sons Ltd;
Anita Hewett: for *The Bird that Wore Stripes* and *Red Umbrella
and Yellow Scarf* from "The Anita Hewett Animal Story Book,"
reprinted by permission of The Bodley Head.

Stories adapted from traditional sources are as follows:

*The Huntress, the Mouse, and the Sun, The Little Bull Calf, Little Red Riding Hood,
The Twelve Dancing Princesses, Robin Hood and the Silver Arrow,
The Ostrich and the Hedgehog, The Little Fir Tree, Anansi and the Magic Pot,
Sour Grapes, The Story of Caliph Stork, Thor's Stolen Hammer, The King
who had Donkey's Ears, The Seal Catcher, Po-Wan and the Kuan-Yin,
The Musicians of Bremen, The Story of Sir Gareth, The Pied Piper of Hamelin,
The Flippityflap* and *Thumbelina* are adapted by Eugenie Summerfield.

How the Twins Escaped, The Elves and the Shoemaker and
The House in the Wood are adapted by Peta Rée.

The Lad who went to the North Wind and *The Three Little Pigs*
are adapted by Deborah Manley.

The Publishers would like to thank Eugenie Summerfield for her kind
assistance in the making of this book.

Tick Tock Tales

5

Minute Stories

Illustrated by
Annabel Spenceley

Edited by Sian Hardy

DORSET PRESS
New York

CONTENTS

THE HUNTRESS, THE MOUSE, AND THE SUN   8
Canadian Indian Legend

HOW THE TWINS ESCAPED   13
Brothers Grimm

THE LITTLE BULL CALF   19
British Fairy Tale

LITTLE RED RIDING HOOD   24
Charles Perrault

DON'T CUT THE LAWN!   28
Margaret Mahy

THE TWELVE DANCING PRINCESSES   33
Brothers Grimm

ROBIN HOOD AND THE SILVER ARROW   39
English Legend

THE OSTRICH AND THE HEDGEHOG   44
African Traditional Tale

THE LITTLE FIR TREE   49
Hans Christian Andersen

ANANSI AND THE MAGIC POT   54
Caribbean Folk Tale

SOUR GRAPES   59
Aesop's Fable

THE STORY OF CALIPH STORK   63
Wilhelm Hauff

THOR'S STOLEN HAMMER   69
Viking Myth

THE ELVES AND THE SHOEMAKER   74
Brothers Grimm

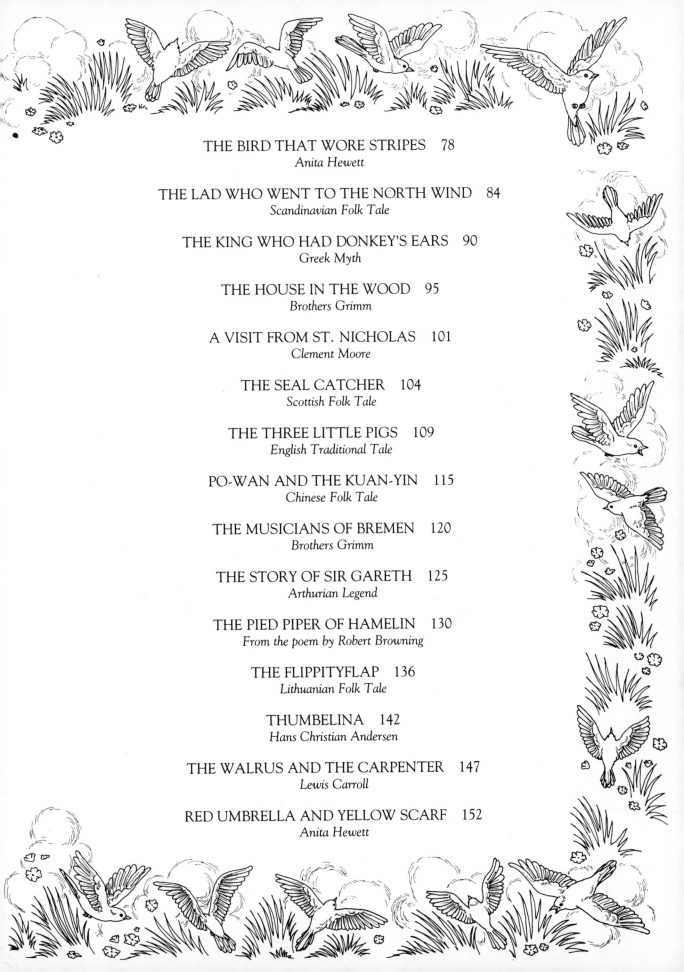

THE BIRD THAT WORE STRIPES   78
Anita Hewett

THE LAD WHO WENT TO THE NORTH WIND   84
Scandinavian Folk Tale

THE KING WHO HAD DONKEY'S EARS   90
Greek Myth

THE HOUSE IN THE WOOD   95
Brothers Grimm

A VISIT FROM ST. NICHOLAS   101
Clement Moore

THE SEAL CATCHER   104
Scottish Folk Tale

THE THREE LITTLE PIGS   109
English Traditional Tale

PO-WAN AND THE KUAN-YIN   115
Chinese Folk Tale

THE MUSICIANS OF BREMEN   120
Brothers Grimm

THE STORY OF SIR GARETH   125
Arthurian Legend

THE PIED PIPER OF HAMELIN   130
From the poem by Robert Browning

THE FLIPPITYFLAP   136
Lithuanian Folk Tale

THUMBELINA   142
Hans Christian Andersen

THE WALRUS AND THE CARPENTER   147
Lewis Carroll

RED UMBRELLA AND YELLOW SCARF   152
Anita Hewett

THE HUNTRESS,
THE MOUSE, AND THE SUN

In the far off days when the world had just begun, there were more animals than people upon the earth. In the land now called Canada, a girl lived alone. She did not mind being alone, for she knew how to look after herself. She had made herself a fine bow and some arrows with which to hunt and she knew how to make a fire to cook on and to keep her warm. So she was quite happy.

When winter came and snow covered the land, food was much harder to find. The girl would watch and wait for the great white snowbirds to fly overhead on their way to the winter feeding grounds. Although it saddened her to have to shoot down these beautiful creatures, they were her only source of food. Every time she shot a snowbird, however, she kept the skin and dried it. Soon, she had collected enough skins to make herself a birdskin coat. It was a fine, warm coat and she was very proud of it.

At last it was spring. The sun shone and the snow slowly melted away. Everywhere, little green shoots appeared through the soil. The distant hills looked inviting in the bright sunshine and the girl wondered if there were people living on the other side. She made up her mind to find out. So she put on her birdskin coat and set off toward the hills. As the girl walked, the sun beat down on her and she became hotter and hotter. After a while, she was so tired she could not take another step. She lay down beside a large stone near a stream and was soon fast asleep.

While she slept, the sun shone down brighter than ever and her birdskin coat shrank and shriveled in the heat. When the girl awoke and stretched herself, her coat fell to the ground in tiny little pieces. She was so angry with the sun that she jumped up, shouting, "I'll show you. You may be high in the sky, but I'll get you! You'll see!"

Without her beautiful coat she could go no farther, so the girl returned home. There she set to work to make a snare for the sun from a strip of buffalo skin. But when it was finished,

the buffalo snare was not strong enough for what she wanted. So she cut three of her long, black hairs and carefully wove them into a snare instead.

"That will do very well," she said to herself. And, taking her snare with her, she set off once again.

She traveled far across the land until she came at last to the Great Sea in the east, where it was summertime and where the sun rose early. Before it was light, the girl placed the snare where it would catch the sun as it rose up from the water to meet the sky. Then she hid behind a tree and waited.

It was not long before the sun rose majestically from behind the horizon, but when it reached the girl's snare, it was caught and held so tightly it could rise no farther.

The girl ran out of her hiding place, crying triumphantly, "I told you I would get you. *That's* for burning my beautiful coat." And with that she ran away home.

Well, that day there was no light at all upon the earth. All the animals, except the night hunters, stayed hidden in their nests and dens. They were too frightened to come out.

The next day there was still no daylight, nor the next, nor the next... And so it went on. Finally, all the animals held a great meeting to discuss what should be done. A goose flying over the Great Sea had seen the sun trapped in the girl's snare and he told the others what had happened.

"The sun in a trap!" they all cried. "Then it will never be daylight again. What shall we do?"

They decided that someone would have to break the snare to set the sun free. But who would undertake such a dangerous task? The heat of the sun was so great, that whoever tried to get close enough would be badly burned.

After much discussion they agreed that they should draw

lots and the woodpecker was picked to go. Off he flew to the edge of the Great Sea. Closer and closer to the sun he went until he could just reach the snare with his beak. He pecked and pecked at it until his head was burned red by the sun, but the girl's hair was too strong for him to break. Eventually he had to give up, but, ever since that time, the woodpecker in Canada has had a red head.

"Someone else will have to go," cried all the animals when the woodpecker returned.

"Leave it to me," said the mouse. He was king of the animals, for in those far off days he was the biggest and strongest of them all. He set off immediately and, with his long, powerful legs, soon reached the edge of the Great Sea.

At once he began to bite through the snare with his sharp teeth. The heat was terrible. He could feel his back burning and scorching, but he did not give up. He nibbled and nibbled away while all the time he was burning and shrinking in the heat. At last he had nibbled through the very last hair and the sun sailed slowly up into the sky from where it shone down upon the land once more.

How the animals cheered to see daylight again! They prepared a great party to welcome the mouse on his return. When at last he arrived, the animals all crowded around to greet their great hero.

"But what has happened to you?" they cried. Alas, the brave mouse was now so small he could hardly be seen and his beautiful fur had turned ash gray. Ever since then, the mouse has been one of the smallest animals, but because of his courage, the sun has been able to shine and bring daylight to the whole world.

How
The Twins
Escaped

Once upon a time, there were a twin brother and sister who lived in a cottage by the edge of a gloomy wood with their father and a housekeeper.

Now the housekeeper did not like children and, after a while, she began to think of a way to get rid of the twins so that there would be less work for her to do.

One day, a wicked idea came into her head. She decided to send the children to a witch who lived deep in the dark wood. So, calling the twins to her, she said, "You have been such good children that I am going to let you visit my grandmother, who lives in a dear little house in the wood. You will have to help her and do as she says, but she will reward you with the best of everything."

Now the little sister was very wise for her age and, as they set off, she said to her brother, "Let's go to see our own dear grandmother first and tell her where we are going."

When their grandmother heard where the housekeeper was sending the children, she cried, "Oh, my poor children! The housekeeper is not sending you to her grandmother but to a wicked witch. I cannot stop her, but listen to me carefully. You

must be polite and kind to everyone you meet and always share your very last crumb with anyone who needs it." Then she gave her grandchildren a bottle of milk, a piece of ham, and a loaf of bread, and the twins set out for the wood.

Among the thickest of the trees, they came upon an odd little hut. Inside was an ugly old woman with a hunched back and a huge wart on the end of her nose. It was the witch.

"Who are you?" she snarled when she saw the twins.

The twins huddled together in fright, but they answered the witch as politely as they could, "Good morning, Grandmother. Our housekeeper has sent us to help you."

"See that you work hard, then," growled the witch. "For, if I am not pleased with you, I will put you in the oven and cook you. That's what I'll do, my pretty dears!" So saying, she sat the girl down to spin yarn, gave the boy a sieve to carry water from the well and set off into the wood.

When the witch had gone, the girl began to weep bitterly because she did not know how to spin. Suddenly, she heard the sound of many little feet and, from every hole and corner in the hut, mice came pattering out.

"Little girl, why are your eyes so red?

If you want help, then give us some bread," they squeaked.

So the girl gave them some of the bread that her grandmother had given her and the mice said that they would spin the yarn. Then they told her that, if she gave the witch's cat some of her ham, it would show her how to escape.

The girl set out to look for the cat, but first she met her brother. He was in great trouble because, no matter how fast he filled the sieve with water, it just poured straight through.

As the girl tried to comfort her brother, they heard a rustle of wings and a flock of wrens flew down beside them.

"Give us some crumbs and do not grieve,
We'll show you water can stay in a sieve," they twittered.

The twins crumbled some of their bread on the ground and the wrens quickly pecked it all up. Then they told the boy to fill up the holes in the sieve with clay. The boy did as he was told and was soon able to fill the sieve full of water without losing a single drop.

When the twins returned to the hut, they saw the cat curled up in a chair. They stroked her, fed her with ham and said to her, "Pussy, tell us how we can escape from the witch."

The cat gave them a handkerchief and a comb and told them to run away as fast as they could. If the witch chased after them, they must throw the handkerchief to the ground. If that did not stop her, then they must throw down the comb.

15

The twins took the handkerchief and comb and set off immediately. First, they met the witch's watchdog. He leaped up at them, barking, but they gave him the rest of their bread and he let them pass.

Next, they came to some birch trees that tried to put out their eyes with their branches. But the girl decorated their twigs with her hair ribbon and the trees let them pass.

Meanwhile, the witch had crept back quietly to see how the children were getting on. She crept up to the window and whispered, "Are you spinning, my little dear?"

"Yes, Grandmother, I am spinning," answered the cat, trying to sound like the little girl.

But the witch was suspicious and went into the hut. When she saw that the twins had escaped, she was very, very angry.

16

"Why did you let the children leave the hut? Why did you help them?" she shouted at the cat.

The cat arched its back and answered, "I have served you all these years and you have never even given me a bone. But the dear children gave me their own ham."

Then the witch scolded the watchdog for allowing the children to escape.

The dog answered, "I have served you all these years and you have never given me so much as a hard crust. But the dear children gave me their own bread."

When the witch scolded the birch trees, they replied, "We have served you longer than we can say, yet you have never even tied a piece of string around our branches. But the dear children decorated us with their own ribbon."

Seeing that she would get no help from her old servants, the witch set off after the twins herself.

By now the twins were very tired and the witch soon began to catch up with them. At once, the boy threw down the handkerchief and, in a moment, a deep, wide river appeared between them and the witch.

It took the witch a long time to find a shallow place to cross the river, but at last she did and she set off after the twins faster than ever.

When the children again heard the witch coming up behind them, the girl threw down the comb. In an instant, a thick hedge grew up. The roots and branches were so closely intertwined that it was quite impossible for the witch to get through. So, gnashing her teeth with rage, she turned around and went back to her hut.

The twins kept on running until they reached their own home. They told their father all that had happened to them and he sent the housekeeper away immediately. From that day on, the children helped their father look after the house and they all lived happily ever after.

THE LITTLE BULL CALF

Long, long ago, there was a boy whose father gave him a little bull calf. Now, because the boy's family was very poor, the little bull calf was more precious to the boy than gold. He loved the little bull calf and fed him with pieces of his own barley bread every day.

One day, the boy's father died. His mother married again, but the man was a cruel stepfather. He hated the boy and threatened to kill both him and the little bull calf. So the boy decided he must leave home, taking his bull calf with him.

They set off early next day and walked for a long, long time, until they were both tired and hungry. When they came to a house, the boy begged a crust of bread. He broke the bread in half and shared it with the little bull calf. At the next house he came to, he was given a little curd cheese. He was going to share this too, but the little bull calf said, "No, you must keep it for later. Soon we shall be going through a dark forest where there are wild beasts and a fiery dragon. I will kill the wild beasts, but the dragon will kill me."

"No, no!" cried the boy, flinging his arms around the little bull calf's neck. "He can't kill you."

19

"Yes, it must be so," insisted the calf. "But you must not be sad. This is what you must do. As soon as we reach the forest, climb up into the tallest tree you can find. You will be safe there from all the wild animals, except the monkeys. If they come after you, the curd cheese will save you. When the dragon has killed me, he will go back to his lair to rest; while he is gone, you must cut out one of my ribs. With this, you will be able to kill the dragon. Hit him with it and he will fall down dead. Then you must remember to cut out his tongue."

The boy did everything the little bull calf had told him. He climbed the tallest tree he could find and when the monkeys chased after him, he held up the curd cheese in his fist and said, "If you come any nearer, I will squeeze your heart as easily as I squeeze this stone."

The monkeys, seeing juice dripping from what they thought was a stone, all turned tail and ran away.

Meanwhile, the little bull calf was fighting all kinds of savage beasts in the forest. He won every battle against them, but when the fiery dragon came, the little bull calf was killed.

The boy waited for the dragon to go. Then he slid down the tree, cut out one of the little bull calf's ribs and went after the dragon. He had not gone far when he found a beautiful princess tied to a tree by her hair. No sooner had the boy set her free than he heard the dragon come roaring toward them.

The boy waited until he could feel the dragon's fiery breath on his face. Then, with a mighty blow, he hit the dragon with the little bull calf's rib and the dragon fell down dead. As it fell, the dragon opened its great jaws and bit off the little finger on the boy's right hand. But the boy still remembered to cut out the dragon's tongue. Bidding the princess farewell, the boy then set off to seek his fortune. But before he left, the princess gave him her diamond ring as a parting gift.

It was not long before the old king came to the forest. He was weeping bitterly, for he was sure that his daughter had been eaten by the dragon. Imagine his surprise and joy to find her alive and unharmed!

On their way back to the palace, the princess told her father how she had been saved by the boy.

"We must find this young man so that he can be rewarded," declared the king.

Messengers were sent throughout the land to find the young man who had a little finger missing, the princess's diamond ring and a dragon's tongue. Whoever could show the king all these three things would marry the princess and one day become king.

Hundreds of men, young and old, flocked to the palace. Many had a finger missing, some on their right hand, some on their left. Many also had rings, some set with diamonds and others set only with pieces of colored glass. Many even brought the tongue of a wild animal. But not one of them brought a dragon's tongue, so they were all turned away.

At last the boy himself came, looking so worn and ragged that the king thought he was a beggar and ordered him to be sent away. Luckily, the princess was standing at her window and saw the boy leaving. She ran to the king, crying, "Father! He is the boy who saved me and killed the dragon!"

The king could hardly believe his ears. Surely this beggar was not the one! But he said, "Let him return and show me the missing finger on his right hand, your diamond ring and the tongue of the fiery dragon."

The boy was brought back to the palace at once and he showed the king all three things.

And so the boy married the beautiful princess and there was much rejoicing throughout the land. When the old king died, the boy became king in his place and ruled his country wisely. But he never forgot his beloved little bull calf, to whom he owed all his good fortune.

LITTLE RED RIDING HOOD

Once upon a time, in a cottage on the edge of a dark forest, there lived a woodcutter, his wife and their little girl. The little girl always wore a warm, red cape with a hood which her grandmother had made for her, so people called her Little Red Riding Hood. Everyone loved Little Red Riding Hood, especially her grandmother.

Early one morning, Little Red Riding Hood's mother said to her, "I want you to take this basket of food to your grandmother as she is not very well. I have put butter, eggs, and a freshly baked cake in the basket, so carry it carefully. Go straight there and always keep to the path. And promise me you won't talk to any strangers on the way."

Little Red Riding Hood promised. Then she put on her cape and, carrying the basket carefully, she set off for her grandmother's house on the other side of the forest.

Little Red Riding Hood had not gone very far when she saw some flowers growing a little way away from the path. She knew her grandmother loved flowers, so she left the path and went to pick some. Just then, a wolf came by. Little Red Riding Hood did not know that he was a wicked wolf. He was also a very hungry wolf and was going to eat Little Red Riding Hood all up. But first he decided to talk to her for a little while.

"Good morning, Little Red Riding Hood," he said in a silky voice. "Where are you going so early?"

"I'm taking some food to my grandmother because she is not very well," replied Little Red Riding Hood.

"Where does your grandmother live?" asked the cunning wolf. He was so hungry that he thought he would eat the little girl *and* her grandmother.

"She lives in the house at the end of the path, by the big oak tree," said Little Red Riding Hood.

The wolf walked along beside Little Red Riding Hood for a while, then he said, "Make sure you pick plenty of flowers for your grandmother, my dear. I must be on my way." And with that he disappeared into the forest.

Little Red Riding Hood carried on picking flowers. Each time she picked one, she saw an even prettier one just a little farther away. And she went deeper and deeper into the forest.

Meanwhile, the wolf had gone straight to Grandmother's house and knocked on her door.

"Who's there?" called Grandmother in a frail voice.

"It's Little Red Riding Hood," answered the wolf, making his voice as soft and sweet as he could. "I've brought you a cake and other good things. Open the door and let me in."

"Lift up the latch and come in," called Grandmother.

So the wolf lifted up the latch and went in. No sooner was he inside the door than he gobbled Grandmother down whole—without even chewing her! Then he put on Grandmother's shawl and nightcap and got into bed. He pulled the bedclothes up to his chin and waited for Little Red Riding Hood.

Presently, Little Red Riding Hood arrived at her grandmother's house and knocked on the door.

"Who's there?" called the wolf in a trembly voice, trying to sound like Little Red Riding Hood's grandmother.

"It's Little Red Riding Hood, Grandmother. I've brought you some presents," said the little girl.

"Then lift up the latch and come right in, my dear," called the wolf, still trying to sound like Grandmother.

Little Red Riding Hood walked in. There was her grandmother in bed. But how strange she looked!

"Grandmother," exclaimed Little Red Riding Hood, "what big ears you have!"

"All the better to hear you with, my dear," said the wolf.

"Grandmother, what big eyes you have!"

"All the better to see you with, my dear."

"And Grandmother, what big teeth you have!"

"All the better to eat you with," growled the wolf and he sprang out of bed to gobble her up. But Little Red Riding Hood just managed to dodge out of his reach.

"Help! Help!" she screamed, as loudly as she could.

Now it happened that Little Red Riding Hood's father was nearby chopping wood. He heard the call for help and rushed to the rescue. He burst into the house and, in an instant, cut off the wolf's head with his ax. Out came grandmother, looking a little bit shaky, but otherwise unhurt. Little Red Riding Hood hugged and kissed her with joy at seeing her alive.

Grandmother was soon quite well again. As for Little Red Riding Hood, she never again strayed from the path, and she was always particularly careful not to talk to any strangers.

DON'T
CUT THE LAWN!

Mr. Pomeroy went to his seaside cottage for a vacation. The sea was right, the sand was right, the sun was right, the salt was right. But outside his cottage the lawn had grown into a terrible, tussocky tangle. Mr. Pomeroy decided that he would have to cut it.

He got out his lawnmower, Snapping Jack.

"Now for some fun!" said Snapping Jack. "Things have been very quiet lately. I've been wanting to get at that cheeky grass for weeks and weeks."

Mr. Pomeroy began pushing the lawnmower, and the grass flew up and out. However, he had gone only a few steps when out of the tangly, tussocky jungle flew a lark crying:

"Don't cut the lawn, don't cut the lawn!

You will cut my little nestlings which have just been born."

Mr. Pomeroy went to investigate and there, sure enough, were four baby larks in a nest on the ground.

"No need to worry, Madam!" cried Mr. Pomeroy to the anxious mother. "We will go around your nest and cut the lawn farther away."

So they went around the nest and started cutting the lawn farther away.

28

"Now for it!" said Snapping Jack, snapping away happily. But just then out jumped a mother hare crying:

"Don't cut the lawn, don't cut the lawn!
You will cut my little leveret which has just been born."

Mr. Pomeroy went to investigate and there, sure enough, was a little brown leveret, safe in his tussocky form.

"We'll have to go farther away to do our mowing," Mr. Pomeroy said to Snapping Jack. So they went farther away and Mr. Pomeroy said, "Now we'll really begin cutting this lawn."

"Right!" said Snapping Jack. "And we'll have no mercy on it."

But they had only just begun to have no mercy on the lawn when a tabby cat leaped out of the tussocky tangle and mewed at them:

"Don't cut the lawn, don't cut the lawn!
You will cut my little kittens which have just been born."

Mr. Pomeroy went to investigate, and there, sure enough, were two stripy kittens in a little, golden, tussocky, tangly hollow.

"This place is more like a zoo than a lawn," grumbled Snapping Jack. "We'll go further away this time, but you must promise to be hardhearted or the lawn will get the better of us."

"All right! If it happens again I'll be very hardhearted," promised Mr. Pomeroy.

They began to cut where the lawn was longest, lankiest, tangliest, and most terribly tough and tussocky.

"I'm not going to take any notice of any interruptions this time," he said to himself firmly.

"We'll really get down to business," said Snapping Jack, beginning to champ with satisfaction.

Then something moved in the long, lank, tussocky tangle.

Something slowly sat up and stared at them with jeweled eyes. It was a big mother dragon, as green as grass, as golden as a tussock. She looked at them and she hissed:

"Don't cut the lawn, don't cut the lawn!
You will cut my little dragon who has just been born."

There, among the leathery scraps of the shell of the dragon's egg, was a tiny dragon, as golden and glittering as a bejeweled evening bag. It blew out a tiny flame at them, just like a cigarette lighter.

"Isn't he clever for one so young!" exclaimed his loving mother. "Of course I can blow out a very big flame. I could burn all this lawn in one blast if I wanted to. I could easily scorch off your eyebrows."

"Fire restrictions are on," croaked the alarmed Mr. Pomeroy.

"Oh, I'm afraid that wouldn't stop me," said the dragon. "Not if I were upset about anything. And if you mowed my baby I'd be very upset. I'd probably breathe fire hot enough to melt a lawnmower!"

"What do *you* think?" Mr. Pomeroy asked Snapping Jack.

"Let's leave it until next week," said Snapping Jack hurriedly. "We don't want to upset a loving mother, do we? Particularly one that breathes fire!"

So the lawn was left alone and Mr. Pomeroy sat on his verandah enjoying the sun, or swam in the sea enjoying the salt water, and day by day he watched the cottage lawn grow more tussocky and more tangly. Then, one day, out of the tussocks and tangles flew four baby larks which began learning how to soar and sing as larks do. And out of the tussocks and tangles came a little hare which frolicked and frisked as hares do. And out of the tussocks and tangles came two stripy kittens which pounced and bounced as kittens do. And *then* out of the tussocks and tangles came a little dragon with golden scales and eyes like stars, and it laid its shining head on Mr. Pomeroy's knee and told him some of the wonderful stories that only dragons know. Even Snapping Jack listened with interest.

"Fancy that!" he was heard to remark. "I'm glad I talked Mr. Pomeroy out of mowing the lawn. Who'd ever believe a tussocky, tangly lawn could be home to so many creatures. There's more to a lawn than mere grass, you know!"

And Mr. Pomeroy, the larks, the leveret, the kittens, and the little dragon all agreed with him.

THE TWELVE DANCING PRINCESSES

Once upon a time, there were twelve beautiful princesses. Every night when they went to bed, their bedroom door was firmly locked, but every morning when they came down to breakfast, their shoes were worn right through, as if they had been dancing all night long. Nobody in the palace could explain how this happened.

At last the king made it known throughout the land that the man who uncovered the princesses' secret could marry the princess of his choice. But anyone who failed to find out the answer after three days and nights would be put to death.

It was not long before a prince came to the palace to try his luck. He was sure that he would be able to find out the secret. That evening, he was taken to the room next to the princesses' bedroom so that he could keep a watch over them. But, in no time at all, the prince fell fast asleep. When he woke up next morning, all the princesses' shoes were worn right through, just as before. The same thing happened on the second night and on the third. So the king ordered his head to be cut off.

Other young princes came, but they were no more successful than the first one. They too were all put to death.

Now it so happened that a soldier who had been wounded and could no longer serve in the army was passing through that country. He met an old woman on the road, who asked him where he was going.

"I'm not sure," he replied with a laugh. "Perhaps I'll go and find out how the princesses wear out their shoes every night. Then maybe one day I'll be king."

To his surprise, the old woman replied, "That's easy enough. Don't drink the wine that will be brought to you in the evening. But you must pretend to fall asleep."

Then she gave the soldier a cloak, saying, "When you put this on, you will become invisible and you will be able to follow the princesses wherever they go."

After listening to the old woman's advice, the soldier decided to try his luck as a suitor for one of the princesses and he made his way to the royal palace.

That evening, when he had been shown to his room, the eldest princess brought him a goblet of wine. But the soldier had remembered the old woman's advice and, hidden under his beard, was a sponge. When he lifted the goblet to his lips, he let the wine run down into the sponge and did not drink a single drop. Then he went to bed and pretended to fall asleep, snoring very loudly.

The princesses laughed when they heard him, but the eldest said, "I wish he did not have to die like all the others."

Then all twelve dressed themselves in their beautiful party clothes, twirling and skipping excitedly in front of the mirror. Only the youngest said, "I'm afraid all is not well."

"Don't be silly!" retorted the eldest princess. "You worry too much; nothing can go wrong. The soldier is fast asleep; just listen to him snoring."

With that she tapped three times on the end of her bed and the bed sank through an opening in the floor. A flight of stairs appeared and, led by the eldest, the princesses went down one after another.

At once the soldier jumped up, threw on the cloak to make himself invisible and followed behind the youngest princess. But, halfway down, he trod on the hem of her dress.

"Someone's grabbed hold of my dress," she cried out.

"Silly girl!" replied the eldest. "It was only a nail sticking out of the wall."

Down they went until they came to a beautiful avenue of trees with silver leaves that gleamed in the moonlight. The soldier, wanting to take back a token, broke off a twig. There was a sharp crack as he did so and again the youngest princess cried out, "Did you hear that?"

"It's only the fireworks to signal our arrival," replied the eldest princess.

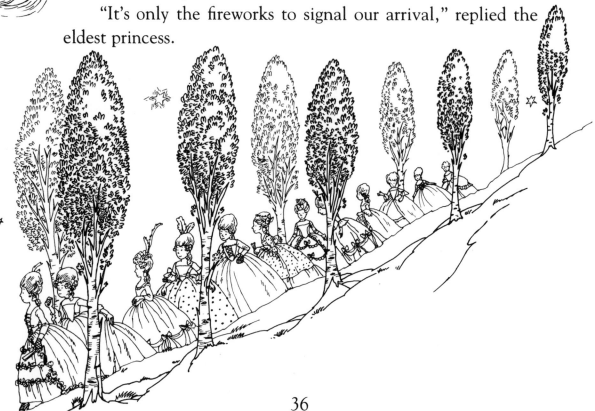

Soon they came to another avenue where the leaves on the trees were of pure gold, and then another where they were made of diamonds. Each time, the soldier broke off a twig from one of the trees and, each time, the youngest princess cried out. But the eldest princess always insisted it was only the fireworks.

At last they came to a lake where twelve boats and twelve princes were waiting for the princesses. Each princess got into a boat and the soldier stepped into the same boat as the youngest. The prince who was rowing wondered why the boat was so much heavier than usual.

On the far side of the lake was a magnificent castle from which came the sound of music. The princes and princesses went inside and the soldier watched as they danced until early morning. Then the princes rowed the princesses home across the lake. As soon as they had reached the other side, the soldier jumped out of the boat and ran on ahead, so that when the princesses tiptoed back into their room, they heard him snoring and thought they were safe. They took off their fine clothes, put their worn shoes under their beds and fell asleep.

Next morning, the soldier said nothing because he wanted to see what would happen on the second and third nights. Everything was just as before. But on the third night, the soldier brought back a golden goblet as another token.

The next morning, the king sent for the soldier and asked, "How do my daughters wear their shoes out every night?"

The soldier told him about all that he had seen and showed him the three twigs and the goblet. The king was astonished and asked his daughters whether the soldier had spoken the truth. They had to admit it was so.

Thereupon, as he had promised, the king asked the soldier which of his daughters he would choose for his bride. The soldier replied, "As I am no longer young, I choose the eldest princess to be my bride."

The princess was delighted. She and the soldier were married that very day and they both lived happily ever after.

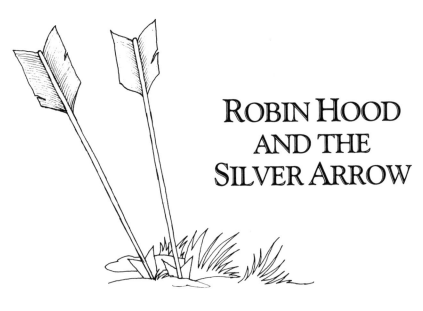

ROBIN HOOD
AND THE
SILVER ARROW

One fine summer's evening, long ago in Sherwood Forest, Robin Hood and his men were sitting under the trees, listening to Alan A'Dale singing a favorite song, when there was suddenly a rustling in the leaves nearby. Alan stopped singing at once and they all fell silent, but when the bushes parted, out stepped their friend Friar Tuck. He had just returned from Nottingham Town with all the latest news.

"The Sheriff is to hold a great archery contest at next week's fair," he told them once he had settled himself down, "and the first prize is to be a silver arrow."

Now the Sheriff of Nottingham was Robin's greatest enemy and it was not safe for Robin or his men to be seen in the town. But the outlaws were not afraid of a little danger.

"Well, my lads," said Robin with a smile. "Who's for Nottingham and the Sheriff's archery contest?"

"I am, Robin!" came voices from all around.

On the day of the contest, Robin and his men swapped their well-known outfits of Lincoln green for countrymen's suits of all different colors so as to be able to mingle unnoticed with the crowds making their way toward Nottingham.

39

The town was thronged with people, all enjoying the fair. Some were dancing around the maypole, others were just wandering around looking at the stalls and sideshows. There were conjurers, jugglers, and even a dancing bear. But the greatest attraction of all was the archery contest.

Robin and five of his most trusted men quietly entered the archery ground and joined the groups of contestants who were waiting eagerly on the sidelines. On a raised platform near the targets sat the Sheriff and his party.

Two blasts on a horn signaled that the contest should begin. Each contestant was allowed three attempts to hit the center of the target. The first man stepped out to shoot, but he shot badly each time. The second contestant was a small man with a wizened face. His three arrows only just missed the center of the target.

"That's a fine marksman," murmured Robin to Littlejohn, who was standing beside him, "I wish he were one of us."

"Perhaps one day he will be," answered Littlejohn.

As the little archer passed, he turned his head and, in that instant, Alan A'Dale thought he recognized him.

One after another the contestants stepped forward and took aim at the target, but none succeeded in hitting the bullseye. At last it was the outlaws' turn. Robin watched with pride as his men proved themselves to be some of the best marksmen in the land. Then Robin himself stepped forward. He fitted an arrow to the bowstring, aimed carefully, and loosed the arrow toward the target. It missed the center by a hair's breadth. Again Robin took aim, and again his arrow narrowly missed the bullseye. The crowd held its breath as Robin took aim for the third and last time. Gleaming like a streak of gold in the late afternoon sun, the arrow flew toward the target and struck it squarely in the center. There was a roar of delight from the crowd and the Sheriff craned forward to get a better look. There was no doubt about it, Robin had won the contest!

The Sheriff's lady stood up to present the silver arrow. As Robin approached the platform to receive his prize, the sun shone full on his face. A man beside the Sheriff leaned forward, stared at Robin and suddenly recognized him.

"It's Robin Hood!" he cried. "Don't let him escape!"

Robin leaped down the steps, sword in hand, ready to face the Sheriff's men.

"After him!" bellowed the Sheriff.

Robin's men were right behind him, swords drawn. In close formation, they moved steadily through the crowd. The Sheriff shouted to the crowd to stand firm, but many had heard of Robin Hood and his pledge to help the poor, and the crowd moved aside to allow the outlaws through. In minutes, Robin and his men were clear of the town and making their way toward the forest, firing arrows back at the Sheriff's soldiers as they went.

But the Sheriff's men soon began to close on them, and Robin feared they would not reach the safety of the forest in time. To his right was the castle of Alan A'Dale's father, Sir Richard, who Robin knew would hide them. But would it be fair to get Sir Richard into trouble with the Sheriff?

At that moment, Littlejohn was hit in the knee by an arrow. They would never reach the forest now. There was only one thing to do. Robin called to his men to help him lift the injured Littlejohn up onto his shoulders and told them to head for the castle. The outlaws cheered as Sir Richard's men lowered the drawbridge for them. But Robin was weighed down by the weight of Littlejohn and was still a long way from the castle. The outlaws continued firing at the Sheriff's men as Robin staggered toward the drawbridge. Just then, a little man with a wizened face ran forward and helped Robin and

Littlejohn to safety. It was the archer from the contest, who was in fact one of Sir Richard's faithful servants. As soon as Robin and Littlejohn were safely across, the drawbridge was raised to the angry shouts of the Sheriff's men.

That night, back in Nottingham, the Sheriff raged and fumed and plotted his revenge. But in Sir Richard's castle there was a huge feast and great celebrations in honor of Robin and all his Merry Men.

THE OSTRICH
AND
THE HEDGEHOG

One beautiful summer's morning, a hedgehog set off for a walk across the sandy desert. He was going to see how far the barley had grown in a nearby barley field. The hedgehog had watched the barley grow from the first tiny, green shoots. Now the stalks were so tall that they towered above his head and the barley would soon be ready for harvesting.

"There's no finer sight than a field of golden barley in the desert," the hedgehog said contentedly.

As he stood on the edge of the field admiring the view, a great, gawky ostrich came striding along. Now ostriches cannot fly, so they have to walk or run everywhere on their strong legs. But they can certainly run very fast.

The hedgehog looked up at the ostrich and called out, "Good morning," in a cheery voice.

But the ostrich merely looked down his nose at the hedgehog and said in a superior voice, "I am not in the habit of talking to stumpy-legged creatures like you."

"My legs may be stumpy," replied the hedgehog, bristling indignantly, "but I can run faster on them than any other animal for miles around."

"Humph!" scoffed the ostrich. "No one can run faster than I can, with my strong, long legs."

The hedgehog's eyes twinkled.

"That's what you think," he said. "Why don't we have a race? Then we'll see who is the faster runner—you or I."

"Oh, it's sure to be me!" boasted the ostrich. "Let's race now, shall we? On the count of three. One, two ...."

"Wait a minute," said the hedgehog. "I haven't had my breakfast yet. I can't run on an empty stomach! We'll meet back here at midday. Then we'll race each other up and down between the rows of barley. Is that agreed?"

The ostrich nodded, thinking that nothing could be easier than racing against such a dumpy little creature. He went off to take a nap, burying his head in the sand as ostriches do.

As soon as the ostrich had gone, the hedgehog raced back home as fast as he could, calling to his family, "Please come quickly, all of you! There's something I want you to do for me in the barley field."

So all the hedgehog's family—mother and father, brothers, sisters, cousins, even aunts and uncles—ran up to the barley field and gathered around him. There he explained to them what he wanted.

"You must help me win a race against the ostrich," he said.

"But how?" asked the other hedgehogs. "You can't hope to beat the ostrich, with his great, long legs."

"I can and I will, if you all listen carefully and do as I ask," replied the hedgehog. "You must all go and position yourselves so that there is one of you at the end of each row of barley. The ostrich and I will start the race at the beginning of the first row, but when he is a few yards ahead of me, I shall turn back. Now, when the ostrich comes racing up to the end of the row, one of you will be sitting there, pretending to be a bit out of breath from running so fast. He will think it is me. Then, when he reaches the end of the next row and sees another hedgehog a bit out of breath, he will think I've beaten him again. And so on."

The hedgehogs thought this was a brilliant idea and they quickly ran off to take up their positions.

At midday, the ostrich returned to the barley field. He was refreshed from his sleep and looked very smug at the thought of winning the race. He lined up with the hedgehog at the start of the first row of barley.

"Are you ready?" he asked.

The hedgehog nodded.

"Then one, two, three—GO!" shouted the ostrich, and off he ran with great strides, smirking to himself and leaving the hedgehog far behind. But when the ostrich reached the end of the first barley row, what did he see? The hedgehog was already there, puffing and panting and calling to him, "Ah, there you are at last."

The ostrich was so surprised he did not reply. Off he ran, even faster, along the next row, but when he came to the end, what did he see? The hedgehog, standing waiting, a little out of breath, but calling, "You've arrived at last."

Again and again the ostrich raced away, running as he had never run before. But each time he reached the end of a row, what did he see? A hedgehog! The ostrich could not tell the difference between one hedgehog and another, so he did not realize that he had seen several hedgehogs—not just one. When he reached the end of the last row, panting and completely exhausted, what did he see? A hedgehog, looking as fresh as a daisy and calling, "So you've made it at last!"

The ostrich could not understand how he had been beaten by a stumpy little hedgehog. He limped off on his tired, sore feet and buried his head deep in the sand. He was so embarrassed at losing the race that he didn't show his face again for a very, very long time.

THE
LITTLE FIR TREE

Long ago, in a far away forest, there once stood a little fir tree. The forest was a lovely place to live—the woodland creatures would play around the little fir tree and the birds would sing as they built their nests in his branches. But the little fir tree was not happy. He had seen the woodman choose the tallest trees in the forest and take them away to become the masts on sailing ships and he wanted to go too.

"I can't wait to grow up," he said. "I want to be the biggest tree in the forest. I want to be a ship's mast and travel all around the world."

"Be happy now," the sun, the wind, and the rain told him.

"Be happy now," sang the birds all around him.

But the little fir tree would not listen to them. He thought he would only be happy when the woodman chose him from among all the other fir trees.

As Christmas drew near, the birds told the little fir tree how the woodman came to choose the best young fir trees to become Christmas trees. The birds described how these trees were taken into houses and decorated with lights and presents. Now the little fir tree wanted to be chosen more than ever.

At last, one Christmas, the little fir tree was chosen. But when the woodman's ax cut deep into his trunk, he felt a great pain and, as he was loaded onto the wagon along with the other young trees, instead of being excited, he was overcome with sadness at leaving his forest home for ever.

After a long and bumpy journey, the wagon was unloaded. The little fir tree heard a man say, "That's a beauty! We'll take that one."

Two men in splendid clothes carried him into a grand drawing room. He felt very important as he was planted in a tub then covered with shining Christmas decorations—toys, parcels, little baskets of candy, and lots of colored lights. A golden star was fixed at the very top. The little fir tree knew he looked beautiful and at last he was happy.

When evening came, the bright lights were lit and the little fir tree sparkled and shone. Suddenly, the drawing room doors were flung open and children rushed in. They danced around the tree gazing with wonder at his beautiful, glittering branches. But soon they were far too busy opening their presents to take any more notice of the little fir tree. Later, a little fat man came and sat down under the tree. He told the children a story about a reindeer called Rudolph. The little fir tree had never heard stories like that before and he looked forward to hearing another story the next day.

But there were to be no more stories and, early one morning, two men came into the room.

"They are going to decorate me again," thought the little fir tree. But he was wrong and, instead, the men carted him off to a shed at the bottom of the garden and threw him down in a dark and dusty corner.

"They are leaving me here for the winter," said the little fir tree to himself, trying to cheer himself up. "I shall be planted again in the spring." But he still felt very lonely.

That night, some little mice crept out of their hole in the floorboards. They danced around the tree, squeaking, "Where do you come from?"

The fir tree told them all about the forest where the sun shone and the birds sang and the great trees grew. He told them about Christmas Eve and how he had been decorated with all kinds of beautiful things.

"How happy you must have been!" said the mice.

Then he told them the story of Rudolph the Reindeer. The mice loved the story. They came the next night to hear it again. And the night after that. But the next night, one mouse said, "Is that the only story you know?"

The little fir tree had to admit that it was and the mice didn't come again. Now the little fir tree was all alone and he thought sadly of his forest home.

"If only I could get out of this place," he sighed. Then, at last, the door opened and some people came in to tidy up the shed. When they saw the little fir tree, they said, "That tree's all brown and withered now." And they tossed him out into the garden. The little fir tree was glad to be out of doors in the fresh air again. Spring had come, and all around flowers were in bloom and the birds were singing. There were children playing in the garden too.

"Now I can be happy again," sighed the little fir tree.

But, alas, he was no longer strong and green and he was put with a pile of garbage ready for the bonfire. On the top of his bare branches the golden star still sparkled in the sunshine. The little fir tree remembered the beautiful summer days in the forest and the winter nights under the stars. He thought of Christmas Eve and how splendid he had looked. He thought too of the story of Rudolph the Reindeer—the only story he had ever heard. As he lay there, one of the children ran up, crying, "Look what I've found!" And he pulled the star from the little fir tree and put it on his coat.

The little fir tree sighed one long, last sigh.

"That was the star I wore on the happiest day of my life. But how soon it was all over."

ANANSI
AND
THE MAGIC POT

On an island in the Caribbean Sea, there once lived a farmer called Anansi. Now Anansi was a lazy man. He could not be bothered to fetch water from the river to make the corn grow and so all his corn dried up. He and his family had very little food and were often hungry, but, instead of working, Anansi spent his days strolling through the forest down to the river, dreaming about food.

Now one morning, as he wandered along down to the river, Anansi saw a beautiful pot with strange writing carved on it lying on the path.

"What a marvelous pot!" he said. "I wonder what this writing means."

"Fill the pot!" answered the pot.

"Fill the pot!" echoed Anansi, amazed to hear the pot speak. He was even more amazed when he saw that the pot was now full of thick, chicken stew. It smelled delicious! Anansi was so hungry he gobbled it all up, sucking the last scraps of meat off the bones.

"That was the best meal I've ever had!" he exclaimed. "But I'm sure this pot can't produce another meal like that."

54

"Oh yes I can," replied the pot. "As often as you wish. All you have to say is, 'Fill the pot!' and I will be filled with any food you want. But you must *never* wash me or you will wash away my magic powers."

"Wash you?" cried Anansi, who had never washed a pot in his life. "Of course I won't wash you!"

Now Anansi was greedy as well as lazy and he made up his mind not to tell anyone else about the magic pot. He would keep it all to himself. So he hid the pot in the long grass, where no one else could find it, and continued on his walk.

Next day, Anansi set off early for his walk. He could hardly wait to find the pot again. He lifted it up and thought of tender roast pork and beans as he said, "Fill the pot!"

At once the pot was full to the brim with a delicious meal. Anansi ate it all, even the pork rind.

That night, Anansi hardly slept a wink. He was thinking of the next meal he would get from the pot.

When at last it was morning, he set off very early and again said to the pot, "Fill the pot!" This time he wished for a rich meat and vegetable stew. Sure enough, the pot was immediately filled with the most mouth-watering meat and vegetables he had ever tasted. Anansi gobbled it all up and then licked the inside of the pot as well.

All this time, Anansi's wife and children had hardly any food to eat. They had to make do with a thin soup made from the few roots they could find in the forest. There was usually only enough for one spoonful each and Anansi always made sure he ate up his share when he came home so that no one would suspect anything.

Anansi began to get fatter and fatter, while his wife and all his children stayed as thin as bean poles. His tummy was soon as big and as round as the magic pot! The children noticed their father's fat tummy and one of them said to his mother, "How come papa is getting so fat when he eats the same as we do?"

"Hush, hush, honey child!" scolded his mother. But all the same, she too began to notice her husband's big, round, pot-like tummy.

"He's up to something," she thought to herself and she decided to find out where he went so early every day.

The next morning, as soon as Anansi had left the house, his wife crept after him, keeping well out of sight. When she saw him eating out of the pot, she was very angry and wanted to teach him a lesson. She did not say anything to him about the pot when he came home that night, but gave him his spoonful of soup as usual.

The very next morning, before Anansi woke up, his wife crept out of the house and ran to where the pot was hidden. She held it up and looked at the strange writing, but she could not

discover what it meant. Looking inside, she thought, "This pot is very dirty. It needs a good wash." So she took it down to the river and gave it a thorough cleaning. Then she thought, "It's a beautiful pot. I will take it to the market and sell it so that I can buy some food," and she set off toward the town.

When Anansi woke up later that morning, he was already thinking about the food he would have from the pot. He was not surprised that his wife had gone out because she often went out early to dig for roots in the forest. He hurried off to where the pot was hidden. But it was not there! He searched and searched. He dug up the earth and pulled up the bushes. But the pot was nowhere to be found. Then he thought, "I know where it is! It must have gone back to the river. A pot that can talk can probably walk as well."

Anansi rushed down to the river. But the pot was not there either. Sadly, Anansi set off home, feeling hungry. There he found his wife with a cageful of chickens and baskets of seeds all ready for planting.

"Where did these chickens and seeds come from?" asked Anansi in surprise.

"Well, it's a long story," replied his wife. "Last night I dreamed that there was a pot not far from here, hidden away and filled with food. When I got up this morning, I went to look for it and I found it."

"Where is it?" demanded Anansi angrily. "What did you do with it?"

"Oh," replied his wife, "you wouldn't believe how dirty it was, so I took it down to the river and washed it. Then I took it to market and sold it. I was able to buy these chickens and these seeds with the money. Now you can look after the chickens and plant the seeds in the field, and soon we will all be able to eat well again, Anansi."

Anansi was furious and would not speak or eat for several days. He got thinner and thinner, except for his big, fat, pot-like belly, which has stayed that way to this very day.

58

SOUR GRAPES

"I'm hungry and I'm thirsty too," sighed Mr. Fox. He had traveled a long, long way that day. His feet were sore, his stomach was rumbling with hunger and his tongue was hanging out with thirst.

He plodded along while the hot afternoon sun beat down upon his back. He had been up since sunrise, hunting in the fields where the early mushrooms grew. Mr. Fox loved mushrooms, but so did many other people. And when Mr. Fox got to the fields, he found that someone had already gathered all the mushrooms and there were none left for him.

"Some creatures are so greedy!" grumbled Mr. Fox. "But I don't care," he said to himself. "I don't even like mushrooms all that much. I'd rather have some fruit instead."

So next he went searching through the woods for wild strawberries. But, although he searched all among the grasses and the leaves, there were none to be found anywhere. Mr. Fox was very disappointed and very cross.

"What greedy things some folk are," complained Mr. Fox. Then he said to himself, "But I don't care. I prefer blackberries to strawberries anyway."

So on he went, nosing around the bramble bushes for blackberries. But he had forgotten it was much too early in the season for the fruit to be ripe yet. There were only one or two small, hard, green berries among the bramble leaves.

"I don't care," snapped Mr. Fox. But this was not true. He did care and he was even more cross and disappointed than before. But he said to himself, "There's better fruit than blackberries to be found elsewhere."

So he carried on walking until the sun began to go down in the sky. Suddenly, he stopped in his tracks, one paw raised. His nose began to quiver as the evening breeze ruffled his golden fur. Mr. Fox sniffed. A delicious smell was wafting toward him from afar. It was the sweet scent of ripe fruit.

"Grapes!" exclaimed Mr. Fox, perking up immediately. "I smell grapes! My favorite fruit!" If his feet had not been so tired and sore, he would have danced with delight.

It was now past sunset and getting dark. A gray and white mockingbird flew overhead on her way to her nest.

"Time to rest! Time to rest!" she called as she flew by.

Mr. Fox yawned. He was now so tired he could hardly put one paw in front of the other.

"I must rest too," he decided.

So he lay down at the foot of the nearest tall tree, curled himself up with his tail over his nose and fell fast asleep, dreaming of the luscious grapes he would have for breakfast.

Early the next day, the mockingbird woke him with her chattering song.

In his most charming voice, the cunning Mr. Fox said, "Good morning, Lady Mockingbird. I'm a stranger in these parts, but I've been told there's a place nearby where they grow some quite good grapes."

"True, very true," replied the mockingbird. "I can show you the garden where the best grapes in the world grow, if you follow me."

Mr. Fox thanked her most politely and trotted after the mockingbird. At last, they came to a large house. Through wrought iron gates, Mr. Fox had a glimpse of the most beautiful garden he had ever seen. It was full of flowers of all colors and bordered by tall, dark cypress trees. But in Mr. Fox's eyes, the best thing that grew there was a great trailing vine that spread along a wooden trellis. Among the green vine leaves hung heavy bunches of ripe, purple grapes.

Mr. Fox was so delighted at the sight of such mouth-watering fruit that he did not even notice that the mockingbird had flown away. He rushed up to the spreading vine and stretched up as high as he could to reach the grapes with his front paws. But, try as he might, he could not reach them.

"I won't give up," he growled. "I'll try again."

This time, he crouched down low then leaped up into the air, grabbing at the grapes with his front paws. But all he got was a pawful of empty air. He rolled back down the bank and landed on his back with a thump.

Again and again he tried, until he was so worn out he could leap no more. With an angry swish of his tail, he turned away from the garden and made his way slowly back down the hill.

"Did you find the grapes?" called the mockingbird from her perch in a tall tree.

"Grapes!" sneered Mr. Fox. "Call those things grapes! I wouldn't eat those if they were handed to me on a silver platter. They looked shriveled and sour to me and I don't care to eat sour grapes, thank you!"

The mockingbird watched Mr. Fox limp slowly away in search of something else to eat. She shook her head and said to herself, "Ah, well. That's how it is with some people. They always pretend they don't want the things they can't have. Sour grapes indeed!"

THE STORY
OF
CALIPH STORK

Long, long ago, there lived a great caliph, or ruler, in the far off land of Persia.

One day, as the caliph rested on his cushions, a sorcerer, disguised as a merchant, came to the palace. He carried a wooden chest with many beautiful things inside it—jewelry, combs, golden goblets, fine silks, and pistols inlaid with gold.

The caliph was dazzled by so many wonderful treasures and he bought the beautiful pistols for his friend and loyal advisor, the vizir. But, just as the sorcerer was about to close the chest, the caliph noticed a small drawer in it and asked to see inside. The sorcerer opened the drawer and carefully pulled out a little box filled with black powder and a scrap of paper covered with strange writing.

"I've no idea what these are," he said, "so you can buy them cheaply, if you wish."

Now the caliph loved old papers and was eager to find out what the strange writing could mean, so he bought the little box for what he thought was a good price. Then he sent for Selim the Scholar, who understood every language in the world, and asked him to translate.

Selim bowed low and began to read, "Whoever takes a pinch of this powder and says, 'MUTABOR,' will be able to turn himself into any animal he wishes and to understand the language of the animals. To return to human form, he must bow three times to the east and repeat the word 'MUTABOR.' But beware! If he should laugh while he is in animal form, he will forget the magic word and will remain an animal for the rest of his life."

The caliph was so thrilled with this discovery that he rewarded Selim with a splendid new coat and made him swear not to tell anyone about the magic powder.

Early next day, the caliph and his vizir set off by themselves. They wandered out of the palace grounds and down to the river bank. A stork was there, searching for frogs, and a second stork was just flying down to land.

"These are interesting creatures," declared the caliph. "Let's turn ourselves into storks."

They each took a pinch of the magic powder and cried, "MUTABOR." In no time at all, their legs became thin and red, their yellow slippers turned into scaly feet, their arms became wings and their bodies sprouted white feathers. They were delighted to be such fine-looking birds.

They listened eagerly to the storks' conversation.

"Good morning, Mrs. Longlegs. You're out early today," said one stork.

"Yes, I'm here to practice my dance," replied the other. With that she twirled and flapped, then tried to balance on one leg. She looked so funny that the caliph and his vizir burst out laughing, scaring the storks away.

"Oh my goodness!" cried the vizir, remembering the warning. "Now we shall be storks for ever!"

"Of course we won't," snapped the caliph. "All we have to do is bow three times to the east and say, 'Mu…Mu…Mu..'"

But both of them had forgotten the magic word.

For several days they wandered about, not knowing what to do. Then they decided that they would fly over the city to see what had been happening while they were away.

To their horror they saw Mirza, the son of the sorcerer, dressed like a caliph and advancing toward the palace. The real caliph and his vizir realized at once that they had been cruelly tricked by the evil sorcerer.

"We must fly at once to the sacred shrine in the east," said the caliph. "Maybe a good spirit there will be able to help us change back into men."

They set off at once, but after a few hours, the vizir could fly no further.

"Let us rest, my Lord," he groaned.

The caliph agreed and the two storks flew down to rest by a ruined castle. As they searched for a place to shelter, they heard the sound of someone crying. The caliph pushed a door open with his beak and there was a brown owl, weeping bitterly. When the owl saw the storks, she cried joyfully, "At last! It was foretold that storks would bring me happiness."

The caliph told her how they had been changed into storks and then the owl told her story.

"I am the only daughter of an Indian king and I have also been bewitched by the evil sorcerer. He demanded of my father that I should be his son Mirza's bride. When my father refused, the sorcerer turned me into an owl and brought me to this ruined castle. Here I must stay until someone asks me to marry him without seeing me in my true form."

Then she went on, "The sorcerer will come here tonight to entertain his friends with stories of his wicked deeds. If you listen outside the doors of the banqueting hall, you might overhear the magic words that will set you free."

So that night, the storks listened behind the door and, sure enough, they heard the sorcerer telling his friends how he had tricked the caliph.

"What was the magic word?" asked the others, laughing.

"MUTABOR," replied the sorcerer.

As soon as they heard the word, the storks flapped away into the open air, being careful not to laugh in their happiness. Then the caliph, turning to the owl, who had followed them, said, "My dear, you have saved my life and that of my best friend. Please will you marry me?"

"Oh, thank you," she replied with joy. "Of course I will." Then the storks bowed to the east three times and cried, "MUTABOR!"

In an instant they were men again, and the owl had changed too—into a beautiful lady with sparkling eyes.

The three set off for the caliph's palace at once. There was great rejoicing at their return and plans were soon under way for a splendid wedding. As for the sorcerer and his son, they were captured and imprisoned in the ruined castle as punishment for their wicked deeds.

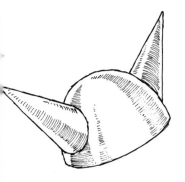

THOR'S STOLEN HAMMER

"Where's my hammer?" roared Thor, the Viking God of Thunder. He had been looking everywhere for his precious hammer, Miolnir, since early morning. Miolnir had been made by a clever dwarf from a meteorite that had fallen from the sky during a great storm. With it and his iron gloves and magic belt, Thor was the most powerful of all the gods. It was he who made the thunder and lightning. It was he who broke up the winter ice so that spring could begin again. So Thor was furious when he found that his hammer had gone.

"Someone must have stolen it in the night," he shouted.

Loki, the mischievous god, heard him and said, "Miolnir must have been stolen by our enemies the giants. I'll go and find out for you." And at once he turned himself into a bird and flew off to the frozen lands of the giants.

Thrym, the King of the Giants, was sitting on a mound of ice, idly tossing snowballs at the trees. He was bored, and even Loki was better than no one at all to talk to.

"What brings you here, Loki?" he asked.

"I am searching for Thor's lost hammer," replied Loki. "Do you know where it is?"

Thrym burst out laughing.

"Of course I do! I took the Thunderer's hammer and I've hidden it deep underground where no one but me can find it."

"But it's of no use to you," said the cunning Loki. "What would you take in exchange for it?"

Thrym smiled, which was not a pretty sight as he had hideously bad teeth.

"Tell Thor that if I can have the beautiful goddess Freya for my wife, I will give the hammer to her as a wedding gift."

Loki flew back to Thor as fast as he could.

"Thrym has your hammer," he reported to Thor, "but he will only give it back if he can marry Freya."

Thor was so eager to recover his precious Miolnir that he rushed off to Freya, shouting, "Freya! Get ready to marry Thrym the Giant, right now."

Freya glared at him and said, "Don't be silly. I am married already. In any case, I would never agree to wed that revolting old giant. How dare you even suggest such a thing!"

Then Thor felt rather ashamed of himself and called all the other gods to a meeting in his father Odin's palace to decide what could be done. The gods all talked for a long time until at last Loki said, "I have thought of a plan. Thrym wants Freya as his bride. If Thor shaves off his beard and disguises himself as a woman, he can go in her place. He can wear a bridal veil and a long white robe adorned with plenty of brooches and jewels."

"Dress as a woman!" roared Thor, banging the table with his fist so that sparks flew. "Never! I would die of shame."

"Nonsense, my son," said Odin firmly. "Loki can go with you as the bridesmaid. The giants will not laugh at you when you have your hammer again and can kill them with it."

So, very reluctantly, Thor agreed to disguise himself as Freya, and with Loki dressed up as the bridesmaid, the pair of them set off in Thor's chariot.

71

Thrym the Giant was delighted when he saw two veiled figures approaching his castle. As he helped Freya from the chariot, he was rather surprised to see how tall she was and what great muscles there were on her arms. But he was too excited to worry about it. Later, when the wedding banquet was served, Thrym was astonished to see his bride eat a whole ox, eight salmon, and several platefuls of cakes. She drank three barrels of mead too.

"I've never seen such an appetite as yours, my dear," he exclaimed. "Do you always eat so much?"

Thor did not know what to say, but Loki answered for him in a high voice, "Freya has been fasting for eight days so that she could look her best for you."

"Bless her little heart!" exclaimed Thrym. "That deserves a kiss." And he leaned forward to raise his bride's veil. Thor was so horrified he sprang up, his eyes flashing.

"My dear, how your eyes flash and flame! What is wrong?" Thrym asked.

Again Loki piped up for Thor, saying, "Freya has not slept for eight days and nights because she was so excited about coming here."

Thrym was as pleased with this explanation as the last.

"Let's get on with the wedding!" he exclaimed. "Bring in my present for the bride."

The hammer Miolnir was carried in and placed upon the bride's lap. At once, Thor seized it and threw off his disguise. With one blow, he slew Thyrm and then any other giant who dared to approach him. The rest fled in terror.

With Miolnir safe in their hands, Thor and Loki rode joyfully back, over the rainbow bridge, to the home of the gods.

Odin had been right. Not one of the giants had laughed at Thor. He had fooled them all.

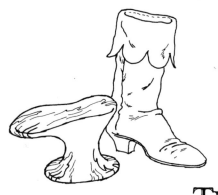

THE ELVES
AND
THE SHOEMAKER

Long, long ago, when fairies danced in the moonlight and goblins worked in the mountains, there lived a poor shoemaker and his wife in a little village at the back of beyond.

The shoemaker was a very honest, hardworking man, but, no matter how hard he worked, he grew poorer every day. At last, he had only enough money left to buy leather for one more pair of shoes. After that he did not know what he would do. That night, he cut out the shoes from the leather so that he could begin work early the next morning. Then he went to bed.

Next day, as soon as it was light, the shoemaker went to his work table. How surprised he was to see a pair of shoes standing where the leather had been the night before! He took up the shoes and looked at them carefully. They were made so well that there was not a stitch or a nail out of place. In fact, he had never seen such a well-made pair of shoes.

A few minutes later, a customer came in. The shoes fitted him perfectly. He was so pleased with them that he paid more than the usual price. Now the shoemaker had enough money to buy leather for two pairs of shoes. That night, he again cut out the leather, ready to work on in the morning.

As soon as the sun was up, the shoemaker went downstairs to set to work. But there, on his work table, were two pairs of shoes, just as beautifully made as the first pair. He sold these almost at once, for nobody had ever had such comfortable shoes before. Now the shoemaker could buy enough leather for four more pairs of shoes.

Once again, the shoes stood finished in the morning. And so it went on until the shoemaker became rich and the fame of his wonderful shoes spread far and wide. All he had to do was to cut out the leather at night and, every morning, the shoes would be standing in a neat row on his work table.

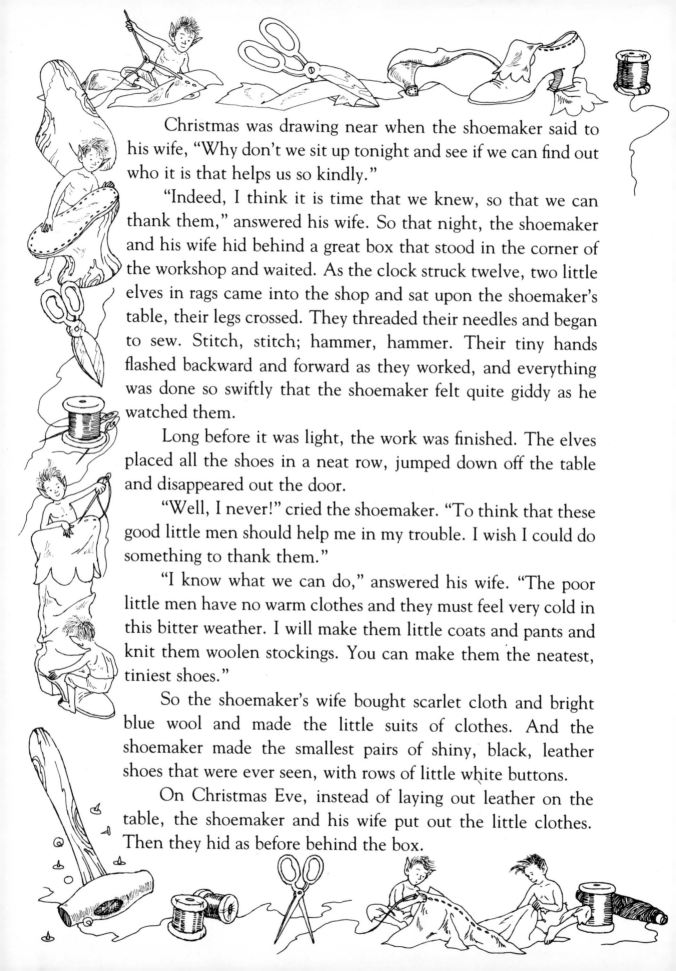

Christmas was drawing near when the shoemaker said to his wife, "Why don't we sit up tonight and see if we can find out who it is that helps us so kindly."

"Indeed, I think it is time that we knew, so that we can thank them," answered his wife. So that night, the shoemaker and his wife hid behind a great box that stood in the corner of the workshop and waited. As the clock struck twelve, two little elves in rags came into the shop and sat upon the shoemaker's table, their legs crossed. They threaded their needles and began to sew. Stitch, stitch; hammer, hammer. Their tiny hands flashed backward and forward as they worked, and everything was done so swiftly that the shoemaker felt quite giddy as he watched them.

Long before it was light, the work was finished. The elves placed all the shoes in a neat row, jumped down off the table and disappeared out the door.

"Well, I never!" cried the shoemaker. "To think that these good little men should help me in my trouble. I wish I could do something to thank them."

"I know what we can do," answered his wife. "The poor little men have no warm clothes and they must feel very cold in this bitter weather. I will make them little coats and pants and knit them woolen stockings. You can make them the neatest, tiniest shoes."

So the shoemaker's wife bought scarlet cloth and bright blue wool and made the little suits of clothes. And the shoemaker made the smallest pairs of shiny, black, leather shoes that were ever seen, with rows of little white buttons.

On Christmas Eve, instead of laying out leather on the table, the shoemaker and his wife put out the little clothes. Then they hid as before behind the box.

As the clock struck twelve, in came the elves. They skipped up on to the table as usual, but when they saw the scarlet coats, the shiny, black, leather shoes and all the other clothes spread out in a row, they shouted with glee. They began to dress themselves as fast as they could, and when they were dressed, they danced together over the chairs and tables, singing with joy:

> *"Smart little elfmen now are we,*
> *Dressed in the best of suits you see,*
> *Never again will we shoemakers be."*

And with that they danced out of the door into the snowy, moonlit night.

The elves never came back after that night, but the shoemaker was now rich enough to pay other people to help him. And everything went well with him and his wife for the rest of their lives.

THE BIRD THAT WORE STRIPES

The chick that wore black and white stripes on his back walked through the grass, and said to himself: "I must find my name, a big, grand name, because when I grow up I shall be a big bird."

He went to the Blue-tongued Lizard, and said: "Please can you help me to find my name?"

"Open your beak," said the Blue-tongued Lizard. "No. Your tongue isn't blue, like mine. So your name isn't Blue-tongued Bird, that's certain. But the feathers grow striped black and white on your back. Perhaps your name is Stripey-feathers."

"Yes," said the chick. "Yes. It might be that. Stripey-feathers!" And off he went.

He stood on the bank of the green lagoon watching long-legged Spoonbill Bird wading among the reeds in the water.

"Hello!" he called. "I'm Stripey-feathers. That's my name. I like it. Do you?"

The big bird looked at the little bird.

"Well, you certainly aren't a spoonbill," he said. "Your beak doesn't look like a spoon. It's stubby. How would Stubby-beak do for a name?"

78

"Yes," said the chick. "I like that, too, I'll be Stripey-feathers Stubby-beak."

Off he went to the edge of the stream, and there he saw Willy Wagtail Bird.

"Hello, Wagtail," he said. "Do you know me? I am Stripey-feathers Stubby-beak."

Wagtail flicked his tail, and said: "I can see your stripes and your stubby beak, but where is your tail? You've forgotten to wear it. Tail-forgotten should be your name."

"Oh!" said the chick. "Perhaps it should. So I'm Stripey-feathers, Stubby-beak Tail-forgotten. That's my name." And he smiled to himself and went to the grassland.

Carpet Snake came sliding along, but he stopped when he saw the stripey bird.

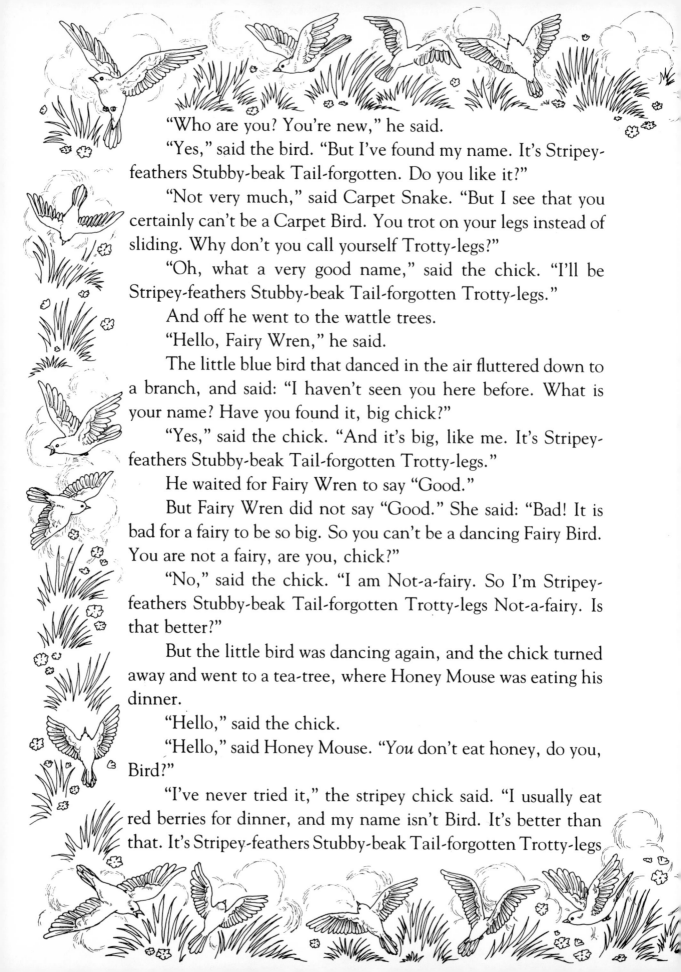

"Who are you? You're new," he said.

"Yes," said the bird. "But I've found my name. It's Stripey-feathers Stubby-beak Tail-forgotten. Do you like it?"

"Not very much," said Carpet Snake. "But I see that you certainly can't be a Carpet Bird. You trot on your legs instead of sliding. Why don't you call yourself Trotty-legs?"

"Oh, what a very good name," said the chick. "I'll be Stripey-feathers Stubby-beak Tail-forgotten Trotty-legs."

And off he went to the wattle trees.

"Hello, Fairy Wren," he said.

The little blue bird that danced in the air fluttered down to a branch, and said: "I haven't seen you here before. What is your name? Have you found it, big chick?"

"Yes," said the chick. "And it's big, like me. It's Stripey-feathers Stubby-beak Tail-forgotten Trotty-legs."

He waited for Fairy Wren to say "Good."

But Fairy Wren did not say "Good." She said: "Bad! It is bad for a fairy to be so big. So you can't be a dancing Fairy Bird. You are not a fairy, are you, chick?"

"No," said the chick. "I am Not-a-fairy. So I'm Stripey-feathers Stubby-beak Tail-forgotten Trotty-legs Not-a-fairy. Is that better?"

But the little bird was dancing again, and the chick turned away and went to a tea-tree, where Honey Mouse was eating his dinner.

"Hello," said the chick.

"Hello," said Honey Mouse. "*You* don't eat honey, do you, Bird?"

"I've never tried it," the stripey chick said. "I usually eat red berries for dinner, and my name isn't Bird. It's better than that. It's Stripey-feathers Stubby-beak Tail-forgotten Trotty-legs

Not-a-fairy. That's my name."

"I don't think it's right," said Honey Mouse. "I'm a mouse that eats honey. I'm Honey Mouse. You're a bird that eats berries. You're Berry-bird."

"Why, so I am," said the stripey chick. "I'm Stripey-feathers Stubby-beak Tail-forgotten Trotty-legs Not-a-fairy Berry-bird. And I think that's enough, for ever and ever."

Off went the chick to the forest trees, and he felt very proud of his big new name.

"I shall tell it to everyone I meet. They will like to hear it," he said to himself.

He met Wombat and Cuscus, but neither of them could

say his name, because it was too long to remember.

The chick stood all alone in the forest, and he felt very sad as he said to himself: "My big new name is just a nuisance. It's much too long for my friends to say. So now I must start all over again, to find a name that is short and easy."

He sighed, and said: "I'm tired of searching. I shall ask the very next creature I see, and whatever they say, that is my name."

Between the trees ran little Brown Rat.

"Rat," called the chick. "Tell me my name."

But Rat took no notice. He ran for his life, squeaking: "Ee ee ee. I must run. Ee ee."

Behind him ran Wild Cat, his long tail waving.

"Cat," called the chick. "I haven't a name."

Cat did not care. He ran after Rat, calling: "Mew. I must

catch him. Mew mew mew."

"Oh dear," said the chick. "They won't even answer. I don't think I'll *ever* find a name."

"Ee," said Rat, as he raced through the trees.

"Mew," said Cat, as he chased close behind.

The chick stretched up on his strong little legs, his beak lifted proudly, his neck very straight. At last he had found his very own name.

"Ee," said Rat.

"Mew," said Cat, far away in the heart of the forest.

"Ee," said the chick.

"Mew," said the chick.

"Ee and mew. That's what they said. So Emu's my name. Emu! I like it."

He kept this new name and liked it, for ever and ever.

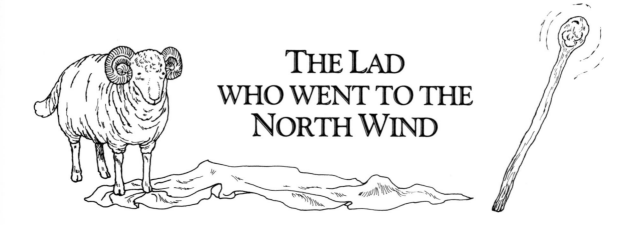

THE LAD
WHO WENT TO THE
NORTH WIND

Once upon a time, there lived a woman and her son called Nils. In their yard they had a little store house where they kept their food and, each day, Nils would go out to the store house to collect porridge oats for their breakfast.

One day, as Nils was coming out of the store house, along came the North Wind. The North Wind puffed and blew until he had caught up all the porridge oats from Nils' bowl and carried them away with him through the air.

Nils sighed and turned back into the store house to fill his bowl again. But when he came out, the North Wind came as before and carried off the oats with a single puff. Now when the North Wind did this a third time, Nils got very angry. He thought it was wrong of the North Wind to treat him in this manner and he decided to go to the North Wind and ask him to give back the porridge oats he had stolen.

He set off at once and, after walking for a very long time, he eventually arrived at the North Wind's house.

"Good day!" called Nils.

"Good day!" replied the North Wind in his loud, gruff voice. "What do you want?"

"I have come to ask you to give back the porridge oats you took from us," said Nils. "My mother and I do not have much to live on and, if you go taking every morsel of food like that, there'll be nothing for us to do but starve."

"I haven't got your oats anymore," said the North Wind more quietly. "But, if you're that poor, I'll give you a cloth that will give you everything you want. All you have to do is say, 'Cloth, spread yourself,' and the cloth will serve up all the food you can eat."

Nils was well contented with this and he set off home with the magic cloth tucked under his arm. As he couldn't reach home before nightfall, he decided to stop at an inn. The people

who were staying at the inn were just about to begin their supper of bread and soup when Nils arrived. Nils sat down at a table in the corner and, laying the cloth over it, said, "Cloth, spread yourself!"

The words were hardly out of his mouth before the table was covered with dishes of tasty meat and vegetables, and plates piled high with jelly and cakes.

Everyone thought the cloth was a very fine thing and the landlady of the inn thought she would like to keep it. So that night, when everyone was asleep, she sneaked into Nils' room, took the cloth and put one of her own cloths in its place. Now because this was just an ordinary cloth, it could not even serve up a piece of dry bread.

When Nils woke in the morning, he took the cloth and set off back home to his mother.

"Where have you been?" she asked.

"I have been to the North Wind's house," replied her son. "He's a good fellow and he gave me this magic cloth. All our troubles are over now we have this!"

"Seeing is believing," said his mother. "First show me what it does."

So Nils proudly put the cloth on the table. Then he took a step back and called out, "Cloth, spread yourself!"

But of course the cloth did nothing.

Nils tried again, but nothing happened.

He tried a third time, but still nothing happened. Eventually he had to give up and that night he and his mother went hungry to bed.

The next day, Nils decided to go back to the North Wind.

"He will surely help us," he said to himself.

It was late afternoon by the time Nils reached the place where the North Wind lived.

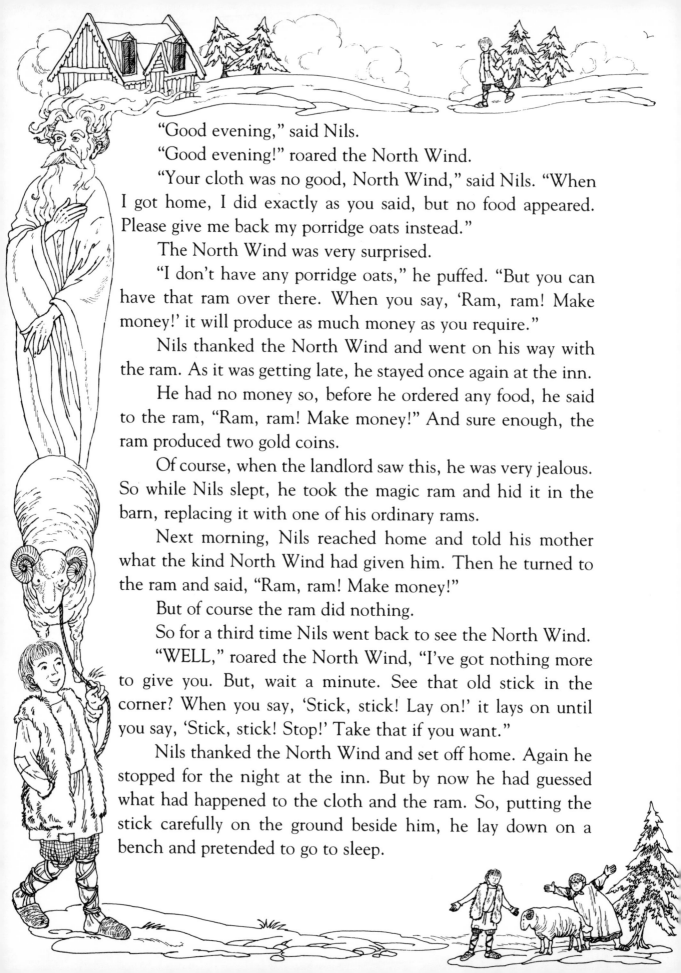

"Good evening," said Nils.

"Good evening!" roared the North Wind.

"Your cloth was no good, North Wind," said Nils. "When I got home, I did exactly as you said, but no food appeared. Please give me back my porridge oats instead."

The North Wind was very surprised.

"I don't have any porridge oats," he puffed. "But you can have that ram over there. When you say, 'Ram, ram! Make money!' it will produce as much money as you require."

Nils thanked the North Wind and went on his way with the ram. As it was getting late, he stayed once again at the inn.

He had no money so, before he ordered any food, he said to the ram, "Ram, ram! Make money!" And sure enough, the ram produced two gold coins.

Of course, when the landlord saw this, he was very jealous. So while Nils slept, he took the magic ram and hid it in the barn, replacing it with one of his ordinary rams.

Next morning, Nils reached home and told his mother what the kind North Wind had given him. Then he turned to the ram and said, "Ram, ram! Make money!"

But of course the ram did nothing.

So for a third time Nils went back to see the North Wind.

"WELL," roared the North Wind, "I've got nothing more to give you. But, wait a minute. See that old stick in the corner? When you say, 'Stick, stick! Lay on!' it lays on until you say, 'Stick, stick! Stop!' Take that if you want."

Nils thanked the North Wind and set off home. Again he stopped for the night at the inn. But by now he had guessed what had happened to the cloth and the ram. So, putting the stick carefully on the ground beside him, he lay down on a bench and pretended to go to sleep.

Now the landlord recognized Nils and, thinking that the stick must be worth something, he went out into the yard and found another stick just like it. Then, when he was sure that Nils was fast asleep, he crept up to swap the two sticks. But Nils was not asleep and he jumped up, crying, "Stick, stick! lay on!"

The stick immediately leaped up from the floor and started to beat the landlord. It beat him until he jumped over the chairs and benches and over the tables. It beat him until he yelled out, "Take back your cloth and your ram, but please take back your stick too!"

Then Nils shouted, "Stick, stick! Stop!"

The stick stopped beating the landlord as quickly as it had started and the landlord went and fetched the cloth and the ram. Nils put the magic cloth in his pocket, led the ram by a string about its horns and took the stick in his hand. Then he set off for home. This time when he showed his mother what the North Wind had given him, all was well.

THE KING WHO HAD DONKEY'S EARS

In the land of Greece in ancient times, there was a king who loved music. Best of all, he loved the music played on the reed pipes by the god Pan. The king thought Pan's music was more beautiful than any other sound in the world, for it spoke of all the wonders of Nature.

There was also a powerful god called Apollo, who thought himself the greatest musician of all. Apollo played an instrument called the lyre, which he played by plucking the strings with a piece of the finest wood. Apollo's music was more solemn and stately than that of the mischievous Pan.

One day, it was decided to have a contest between Apollo and Pan to prove who was the best musician. The Great Mountain God was called to be the judge and the king and everyone else came from far and wide to listen to the contest.

First, Pan played his music. It was magical! Even the trees bowed down to hear. Then it was Apollo's turn. The harmonies were so wonderful that they brought tears and cheers of delight from the audience. It was hard to say who was the best musician, but at last, the Great Mountain God declared, "Apollo is the winner."

Everyone was pleased, except for the king, who grumbled to his courtiers, "I think Pan should have been the winner. His music is the sweetest ever heard by human ears!"

Now when Apollo was told what the king had said, he was furious and said, "If that is what the king thinks, he does not deserve to have human ears. When he wakes tomorrow, he shall have donkey's ears."

Sure enough, next day when the king looked in the mirror, he saw that his ears had sprouted up into long, pointed, very hairy donkey's ears.

"This is terrible!" exclaimed the king. "Everyone will laugh at me."

The only way he could hide his donkey's ears was to wear a huge turban that completely covered them. People thought the king had started a new fashion and they started to wear large turbans too.

Soon the time came for the king to have his hair cut. Looking very grim, he went to the royal hairdresser, but, before he removed his turban, he said, "I command you on pain of death to keep a secret. You must never tell a living soul about my ears."

The hairdresser promised and the king took off his turban and allowed the hairdresser to cut his hair. Now it is always very difficult to have a secret and not share it. After a while, the hairdresser longed to tell someone else about the king's ears. But he knew that if he did, he would be put to death.

Then he had a great idea. Early one morning, he went off to a lonely part of the woods and, at the edge of a stream, he dug a hole. Into the hole he whispered his secret: "The king has donkey's ears."

Then he covered up the hole and went away happily, thinking his secret was safe.

After a while, strong reeds grew where the hole had been. They were the kind of reeds from which musical pipes are made. It was not long before some young shepherd boys came and sat by the stream to rest. They cut some of the reeds, made them into pipes and began to play. But, instead of the tunes the boys wanted to play, the pipes sang:

"Hark my dears,
The king has donkey's ears."

The tune floated away on the breeze and was carried throughout the land. Soon everybody knew about the king's donkey ears.

When the king found out that his secret had been betrayed, he was furious. He ordered the hairdresser to be brought before him and called all his people to gather in the palace courtyard. The hairdresser was brought in, trembling with fear. The king was surely going to order his execution!

But when at last the king stepped forward to address his people, he found he was no longer angry.

"Yes, it is true," he said, "I have donkey's ears. But I cannot punish the hairdresser for telling the truth. What does it matter what shape your ears are as long as you enjoy hearing music and songs? Look, I am not afraid to show you my ears." And with that he pulled off his turban.

Everyone gasped and stared. Then they cried, "But, your Majesty, your ears are just like ours!"

And so they were. For Apollo had decided that the king had suffered enough and had removed the magic spell. Now when the reed pipes played, they sang a different song:

"Three cheers
For the ears of our king,
Three cheers
For the king's ears."

THE HOUSE IN THE WOOD

Once upon a time, there was a woodcutter who lived with his wife and three daughters in a hut by a great forest.

One morning, as he was going off to work, the woodcutter said to his wife, "Let Mary bring me my lunch today and, so that she doesn't lose her way in the forest, I will leave a trail of grain on the path."

At midday, Mary set out with some soup for her father. But the birds had pecked up all the grain and the girl could not find her way. As darkness fell, Mary was still lost in the forest and began to feel very frightened. Then, in the distance, she saw a house with lights in the window.

"The people living there will take me in for the night," she thought and she went up and knocked on the door.

"Come in!" called a gruff voice.

She stepped in and saw an old, white-haired man seated at a table. His white beard flowed over the table and almost down to the ground. Lying down by the stove, were a hen, a cock, and a brindled cow.

The girl told the old man her story and asked if she could stay for the night.

The old man turned to the animals and said:

> "Pretty cock, pretty hen,
> And you, pretty brindled cow,
> What do you say now?"

The animals nodded to say that the girl could stay. So the old man said to her, "There is plenty of food. Go into the kitchen and cook us some supper."

The girl did as she was told, and when the meal was ready, she sat down opposite the man and ate until she could eat no more. She never thought to give anything to the animals.

Then she said, "I am tired. Show me where I can sleep." The animals answered:

> "You have eaten with him,
> You have drunk with him,
> Of us you have not thought.
> Sleep then as you ought!"

The old man said, "There is a bedroom upstairs. Make up the bed and go to sleep."

When Mary was asleep, the old man came up and looked at her by the light of a candle. He shook his head sadly, then he opened a trapdoor and let her fall down into the cellar.

That same evening, the woodcutter came home late and asked his wife why she had not sent Mary with his dinner.

"But I did," she answered. "She must have lost her way."

The next day, the woodcutter asked his daughter Jane to bring his food, and this time he left a trail of lentils. But when Jane set out at midday, the birds had pecked up all the lentils and Jane soon became lost.

After wandering about for a long time, she came to the old man's house and asked for food and a night's lodging.

The white-haired old man again asked the animals:

> *"Pretty cock, pretty hen,*
> *And you, pretty brindled cow,*
> *What do you say now?"*

Again the animals nodded their consent and everything happened as on the day before. The girl cooked a good meal, but she did not bother to feed the animals.

When she asked for a bed, they replied:

> *"You have eaten with him,*
> *You have drunk with him,*
> *Of us you have not thought.*
> *Sleep then as you ought!"*

Once she was asleep, the old man shook his head sadly over the girl, then let her fall into the cellar to join her sister.

On the third day, the woodcutter said to his wife, "Send Anne today with my dinner. She is always obedient and will keep to the right path and not wander away like her sisters."

The mother did not want Anne to go, but her husband said, "Don't worry, she is too clever to lose her way, and I will take plenty of peas with me to make a trail for her."

But when Anne set out, the wood pigeons had eaten up all the peas, and she was soon lost in the forest. Anne was very upset to think of her poor, hungry father and her worried mother, but she could not find her way.

At last, when it was dark, she too came to the house in the wood and asked if she might stay the night.

The old man again asked the animals:

> "Pretty cock, pretty hen,
> And you, pretty brindled cow,
> What do you say now?"

And once again they nodded to say yes. Anne stepped up to where they were lying and stroked the cock and the hen, and scratched the brindled cow between its horns.

When she had cooked a good supper and put the dishes on the table, she said, "But I cannot eat a good meal while the dear animals have nothing. I will attend to them first."

She went into the yard and fetched barley for the cock and hen, and brought the cow an armful of sweet-smelling hay.

"Eat that, dear animals," she said, "and when you are thirsty, I will fetch you some water."

When the animals had eaten and drunk their fill, Anne sat down opposite the old man and ate her supper.

As the animals began to settle down for the night, they said to the girl:

> "You have eaten with us,
> You have drunk with us,
> You have cared for us right,
> So we wish you good night."

Then Anne went upstairs and was soon fast asleep.

When she awoke in the morning, what a sight met her eyes! She was lying in a beautiful room furnished with great splendor. The walls were papered with gold, the bed was made of the finest wood and the quilt was made of velvet. On a stool by the bed lay a pair of slippers, covered with pearls.

As the girl lay in bed, thinking she must be dreaming, three servants came in and asked what they could do for her.

99

"Nothing," said Anne. "I must get up at once and cook a meal for the old man and feed the animals."

But, just then, the door opened and in came a handsome young man.

"I am a king's son," he said. "But a wicked witch put a spell on me and I was turned into an old man, while my three faithful servants were turned into a cock, a hen, and a brindled cow. The spell could only be broken by a girl who was kind, not only to an old man, but also to his animals. You are that girl, and last night the spell was broken and this house was changed back into my royal palace."

Then the prince asked Anne to marry him, and when she agreed, he sent his three servants to fetch her parents.

"But where can my sisters be?" asked Anne.

"Do not worry about them," replied the prince. "They are safe in the cellar and will be taken to live on a farm where they can learn to be kind to animals."

A VISIT FROM ST. NICHOLAS

Twas the night before Christmas, when all
through the house
Not a creature was stirring, not even a mouse;
The stockings were hung by the chimney with care,
In hopes that St. Nicholas soon would be there;
The children were nestled all snug in their beds,
While visions of sugar-plums danced in their heads;
And mamma in her 'kerchief, and I in my cap,
Had just settled down for a long winter's nap—
When out on the lawn there arose such a clatter,
I sprang from my bed to see what was the matter.
Away to the window I flew like a flash,
Tore open the shutters, and threw up the sash.
The moon, on the breast of the new-fallen snow,
Gave the luster of midday to objects below;
When, what to my wondering eyes should appear,
But a miniature sleigh and eight tiny reindeer,
With a little old driver, so lively and quick,
I knew in a moment it must be St. Nick.

More rapid than eagles his coursers they came,
And he whistled, and shouted, and called them by name:
"Now, *Dasher!* now, *Dancer!* now, *Prancer* and *Vixen!*
On, *Comet!* on, *Cupid!* on, *Donner* and *Blitzen!*
To the top of the porch! to the top of the wall!
Now dash away! dash away! dash away all!"
As dry leaves that before the wild hurricane fly,
When they meet with an obstacle, mount to the sky;
So up to the house-top the coursers they flew
With the sleigh full of toys, and St. Nicholas too.
And then, in a twinkling, I heard on the roof
The prancing and pawing of each little hoof—
As I drew in my head, and was turning around,
Down the chimney St. Nicholas came with a bound.
He was dressed all in fur, from his head to his foot,
And his clothes were all tarnished with ashes and soot;
A bundle of toys he had flung on his back,
And he looked like a pedlar just opening his pack.
His eyes—how they twinkled; his dimples, how merry!

His cheeks were like roses, his nose like a cherry!
His droll little mouth was drawn up like a bow,
And the beard of his chin was as white as the snow;
The stump of a pipe he held tight in his teeth,
And the smoke it encircled his head like a wreath;
He had a broad face and a little round belly
That shook, when he laughed, like a bowl full of jelly.
He was chubby and plump, a right jolly old elf,
And I laughed when I saw him, in spite of myself;
A wink of his eye and a twist of his head
Soon gave me to know I had nothing to dread;
He spoke not a word, but went straight to his work,
And filled all the stockings; then turned with a jerk,
And laying his finger aside of his nose,
And giving a nod, up the chimney he rose;
He sprang to his sleigh, to his team gave a whistle,
And away they all flew like the down of a thistle.
But I heard him exclaim, ere he drove out of sight,
"*Happy Christmas to all, and to all a good night!*"

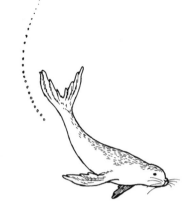

THE
SEAL CATCHER

In a wild and lonely place on the rocky coast of Scotland, there once lived a man who made his living by catching seals and selling their skins.

One sunny day, the seal catcher came out of his cottage and saw a large seal on the rocks below. Thinking of all the money he could earn from such a fine seal skin, he crept down towards the seal and leaped upon it with his knife.

The rocks were covered with slimy seaweed and the seal catcher slipped just as he stabbed at the seal. With a scream of pain, the seal dived back into the water with the seal catcher's hunting knife still sticking into its side.

The seal catcher set off home, feeling annoyed at having lost the seal, not to mention his hunting knife. On the way, he met a tall, richly dressed stranger on a magnificent gray horse. He stood aside to let the stranger pass, but, to his surprise, the stranger stopped and asked him what his trade was.

"I'm a seal catcher," he replied. At once, the stranger ordered a hundred seal skins. The seal catcher was delighted at his good fortune until the stranger said, "You must deliver all the seal skins to me tonight."

"But that's impossible!" cried the seal catcher. "The seals won't come back to the rocks again until tomorrow morning. And besides, I have lost my best hunting knife."

"Never mind about that," replied the stranger. "Get up behind me on my horse. I'll take you to where there are hundreds of seals and I'll give you a new knife too."

So the seal catcher got up on the horse behind the stranger and away they went. They rode so fast that they seemed to fly through the air. Suddenly, they came to a stop. They had reached the edge of a steep cliff. Dismounting, they looked down at the foaming sea far below.

The seal catcher looked anxiously around and asked, "Where are the seals you told me about?" He began to feel afraid of the tall stranger and tried to run from him. But the stranger caught him in a firm grip and leaped with him over the cliff edge. Together they plunged down into the sea.

The seal catcher found they were in a strange underwater world where he could breathe as easily as if he were on dry land. He saw that the stranger had changed into a seal. Then he realized that he too had been transformed into a seal.

"There is a spell on me," thought the seal catcher. "Now I will have to remain a seal for the rest of my life."

The stranger took him through an arch in the rocks into a huge cavern where there were hundreds of seals. They looked sad, and many of them were weeping.

"Wait here," said the stranger. Then he went through a hole at the end of the cavern and returned with a knife.

"Is this yours?" he asked sternly.

"It is," mumbled the seal catcher. "But I was only trying to earn my living."

Now the seal catcher thought he understood why he had been brought here. The seals were going to take their revenge and kill him with his own knife. But, instead, they crowded around him, gently rubbing their soft noses against him.

"Follow me," said the stranger. "They will not harm you."

The seal catcher was led into a small cave where a wounded seal lay on a bed of seaweed. It was the seal he had tried to kill that morning.

"He is their king," said the stranger. "He will die unless you take away his pain."

"I will try," said the seal catcher, who was truly sorry now he realized the hurt he had caused. He stretched out his hand to the seal king and gently touched his wound. As he did so, a terrible pain shot through him, making him cry out. Then the pain slowly died away and the seal catcher saw the seal's wound begin to heal. Soon, not even a scar could be seen and the seal king rose from his bed.

Presently the king said to the seal catcher, "You are free to go home now. But first you must promise never to hunt or harm a seal again."

The seal catcher promised, although he knew it would mean giving up his livelihood. The stranger took him up through the dark sea until they were out in the sunlight once more. Then, with one bound, they reached the cliff top. The gray horse was waiting patiently for them and, in no time at all, the seal catcher was returned to his cottage.

The seal catcher became a farmer after that. He threw away his hunting knife and never hunted seals again, and he enjoyed good fortune to the end of his days.

THE THREE LITTLE PIGS

Once upon a time, there were three little pigs who lived with their mother. One day, she called them all to her and said, "Children, it is time for you to set out and make your own way in the world. But remember! You must always beware of the big bad wolf."

The three little pigs set out immediately. As they went down the lane, they met a man with a load of straw and the first little pig asked him for some straw to build a house.

"Of course," said the man, and he gave the little pig a big bundle of straw.

In no time at all, the little pig had built himself a house and, with a contented grunt, he settled down inside.

The other two little pigs carried on walking. When they met a man with a cart loaded with sticks, the second little pig asked if he could have some sticks to build himself a house.

"Of course, little pig," said the man, and he gave the little pig a bundle of sticks.

The little pig worked hard to build himself a house of sticks. When at last it was finished, he lay down inside and grunted happily.

Meanwhile, the third little pig had continued on down the road. On his way, he met a man with a barrow loaded with bricks and he thought, "It will be hard work to build a house of bricks, but it will be a very strong house." So he asked the man if he could have some bricks.

"Certainly, little pig," said the man, and together they unloaded some bricks into a pile at the side of the road.

The little pig worked hard all that day and the next. His brothers came to watch him and poked fun at him for wanting a house made of bricks. But the third little pig ignored them and carried on working until at last his house was finished.

The very next day, who should come loping along the road but the big bad wolf. When he saw the little house made of straw, he stopped and sniffed the air. He could smell the smell of young pig and he crept up to the house of straw.

"Little pig, little pig," he called out, "let me come in."

But the little pig recognized the voice of the big bad wolf.

He called out from inside his straw house, "No, no! By the hair of my chinny-chin-chin, I'll not let you in."

So the big bad wolf shouted, "Then I'll huff and I'll puff and I'll blow your house in." And he huffed and he puffed and the straw flew in every direction. The little pig only just managed to escape and he ran as fast as his legs would carry him to his brother's house made of sticks. Rushing inside, he cried, "Help, help! The big bad wolf is after me." So the second little pig slammed the door of his house and locked it.

The big bad wolf loped along the road after the little pig. When he saw the house made of sticks, he stopped and sniffed the air. This time, he could smell the smell of two young pigs and, creeping up to the house made of sticks, he called out, "Little pigs, little pigs, let me come in."

The two little pigs shook and shivered inside the house, but they called out to him, "No, no! By the hair of our chinny-chin-chins, we'll not let you in."

"Then I'll huff and I'll puff and I'll blow your house in," shouted the big bad wolf. And he huffed and he puffed, and he puffed and he huffed until the house of sticks collapsed.

The two little pigs just managed to escape out of the back door. They ran as fast as their legs would carry them to their brother's house made of bricks. Rushing inside, they panted, "Help, help! The big bad wolf is after us!" So the third little pig slammed the door of his house and shut all the windows.

Soon, the big bad wolf came loping down the road. But when he came to the house made of bricks, he stopped and sniffed the air.

"My goodness!" he exclaimed. "I can smell the smell of *three* young pigs!" And he crept up to the house and called out, "Little pigs, little pigs, let me come in."

The three little pigs shook and shivered inside the house, but they shouted back, "No, no! By the hair on our chinny-chin-chins, we'll not let you in!"

"Then I'll huff and I'll puff and I'll blow your house in," shouted the big bad wolf.

So he huffed and he puffed, and he puffed and he huffed, but nothing happened. So he huffed and he puffed, and he puffed and he huffed again, but still nothing happened. The little house stood as firm as a rock.

The exhausted wolf slunk off into the woods to think of another way to catch the three little pigs. After a lot of thinking, he had an idea and rushed back to the brick house.

"Little pigs," he called, "there are some lovely turnips in the farmer's field. Let's go and collect some tomorrow."

Now the three little pigs liked turnips very much, so the third little pig called out, "All right, Mr. Wolf, I'll meet you at the farmer's field at ten o'clock."

Next morning, the little pig got up very early and went straight to the farmer's field. He collected all the turnips he needed and was home before the wolf was even out of bed.

The wolf was furious at being tricked, but he decided to have another go at catching the three little pigs.

"I'm sorry I missed you in the farmer's field this morning," he called outside the little brick house. "There are some lovely juicy apples in the farmer's orchard. Shall we go together at five o'clock tomorrow morning and get some?"

The three little pigs liked apples even more than they liked turnips, so the third little pig called out, "All right, Mr. Wolf, I'll meet you at the farmer's orchard at five o'clock."

Next morning, the little pig got up very, very early, as before. But this time, the wolf came early too. He arrived while the little pig was still up in an apple tree.

The little pig pretended to be pleased to see the wolf and threw him an apple. Then, while the wolf was picking it up, he jumped down out of the tree into a barrel, rolled all the way down the hill to his house and rushed in and bolted the door.

The wolf was so angry that the little pig had tricked him again that he ran all the way back to the little house of bricks. There, he decided to climb onto the roof and come down the chimney to catch the three little pigs. But the three little pigs were ready for him. They had put a cauldron of water on the fire so that, when the wolf came slipping and sliding down the chimney, he fell – Splash! – straight into the boiling water.

"Aaah!" shrieked the wolf and leaped straight back up the chimney in one bound.

After that, the three little pigs lived happily in the brick house for many years. And you can be sure that they never saw the big bad wolf again.

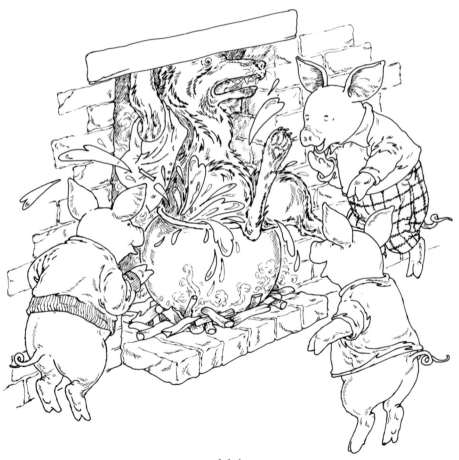

Po-Wan
and
The Kuan-Yin

In China, many years ago, a boy was born into the family of Chin, which means gold. He was named Po-wan, which means a million, because it was foretold that one day he would be rich and have a million pieces of gold.

But Po-wan spent all his money on the poor. He gave away so much that he hardly had any food for himself and his clothes were always worn and ragged.

One day he asked himself, "Why is it that I, who am called A Million Pieces of Gold, have not a coin to give a beggar or a bowl of rice to share with him?" He decided to go and seek the answer from the wise goddess, the Kuan-yin.

Po-wan traveled for many days until he came to a wide and fast-flowing river. As he stood on the river bank, deciding how he could cross, a deep voice called from the hilltop, "Po-wan, are you going to see the Kuan-yin?"

"Yes," replied Po-wan, wondering who was calling to him.

"Then would you ask her a question for me?"

Po-wan knew that he could only ask the Kuan-yin three questions, but, as he had only one of his own to ask, he willingly agreed to the voice's request.

Then a huge snake appeared over the hill. It was so enormous it could easily have swallowed Po-wan up in one gulp. Po-wan trembled with fear.

"Ask the Kuan-yin why it is that, although I am a thousand and one years old, I am not yet a dragon," hissed the snake. "For I am good and never greedy, as you can see."

Po-wan was very relieved to hear this.

"I will ask her," he said. "But how am I to cross this river?"

"I shall take you on my back," declared the snake.

Po-wan hung on tightly to the snake's slippery back as it swam across the river and was very glad to reach the other side. He hurried on his way and soon came to an inn where he stopped and asked for a bowl of rice.

"What brings you here?" asked the innkeeper.

Po-wan told him that he was going to visit the Kuan-yin.

"Then ask her a question for me," pleaded the innkeeper. "My beautiful daughter cannot speak. Please ask the Kuan-yin why this is so."

Po-wan felt sorry for the innkeeper and readily agreed.

After all, the Kuan-yin would answer three questions and Po-wan had only one of his own to ask.

Po-wan traveled on until it was dark. At the next house he came to, he asked if he could have a bed for the night. The house belonged to a rich man who gave Po-wan a good meal and a comfortable bed to sleep in.

Next morning, when Po-wan was about to leave, the rich man called out, "As you are going to the Kuan-yin, would you ask her a question for me? In my garden are many special plants and trees that have been well looked after for twenty years. But none of them will flower or bear fruit. Please ask the Kuan-yin why this is so."

"Of course I will," promised Po-wan without hesitation.

Alas! He was only allowed to ask the Kuan-yin three questions and now there were four. What should he do?

Po-wan knew the answer.

"I have made promises to the Great Snake, the innkeeper and the rich man," he said to himself, "and promises must always be kept."

When Po-wan arrived at the Kuan-yin's temple, she invited him to ask his three questions.

"Why is the Great Snake not yet a dragon when he has been good and never greedy for a thousand and one years?"

The Kuan-yin replied, "There are seven pearls on his head. If he takes six away, he will become a dragon."

Next, Po-wan asked, "Why can the innkeeper's daughter not speak?"

The Kuan-yin replied, "It will be so until she sees the man she will marry."

Then Po-wan asked, "Why are there no flowers or fruit in the rich man's garden?"

The Kuan-yin replied, "There are seven caskets of gold and silver in his garden. There will be no flowers nor fruit until he gives away half this treasure."

Po-wan thanked the Kuan-yin and set off home. First, he gave the rich man the goddess's answer. The rich man was so grateful that he gave Po-wan half his treasure. Next, Po-wan went to the innkeeper to tell him what the Kuan-yin had said. When the innkeeper's daughter saw him from her window, she called out, "Welcome back, Po-Wan!"

The innkeeper was so delighted to hear his daughter speak, he agreed at once to let her marry Po-wan.

Then Po-wan went to the Great Snake and told him what the goddess had said. The snake gave six of his pearls to Po-wan and was immediately transformed into a magnificent dragon.

And that is how Chin Po-wan, through his kindness and goodness, came to be a rich man worth a million gold pieces.

THE MUSICIANS OF BREMEN

There was once an old donkey who was too old for work. One day, he heard his master say, "I can't keep an animal who is no longer useful."

The old donkey said to himself, "I may be too old to carry heavy loads, but I can make a great noise when I bray. I shall run away and earn my living as a musician."

That night, the donkey slipped out of the stable and trotted off down the road toward the town of Bremen. He had not gone far when he saw a sad old dog lying by the roadside.

"Why are you sad, Dog?" asked the donkey.

"You would feel sad too if your master had said he was going to get rid of you because you were too old to hunt any more," said the dog.

"Then come with me, my friend," said the donkey. "I'm off to Bremen to earn my living as a musician. You have a good voice; you and I can sing together."

"Gladly," said the dog.

The donkey and the dog set off together down the road. They had not gone far when they saw an old cat sitting on a gate, looking very miserable.

"Why do you look so unhappy, Cat?" they asked her.

"I cannot catch as many rats and mice as I did when I was young. So my mistress is getting a kitten instead, and I am to be got rid of," replied the cat.

"Then come with us," said the donkey and the dog. "We are going to Bremen to earn our living as musicians. You have a marvelous singing voice. Together we'll make a fortune."

The cat liked this idea, so the three animals went on together to Bremen. Soon they came to a farmyard. A cock was strutting up and down muttering to himself, his feathers all ruffled in anger.

"Whatever is the matter?" the three friends asked.

"I've just heard my mistress say she's going to eat me for dinner on Sunday," replied the cock.

"Then don't stay here any longer," said the donkey, the dog and the cat. "Come with us. We're going to earn our living as musicians. You can come too."

"Cock-a-doodle-doo!" crowed the cock joyfully.

So off they went, all four together. It was too far for them to reach Bremen that day, so, when it began to get dark, the friends took shelter in a wood for the night. The dog and the donkey lay down at the foot of a tree, the cat climbed up into the branches and the cock roosted high up at the top of the tree. As they were settling down, the cock in his high perch spotted a light shining through the trees. He called down to the others, "I can see a light; there must be a house nearby. We might find food and better shelter there. Why don't we go and take a look."

They were all very hungry, so they set off toward the light and soon came to a house. They crept up to it and the donkey, being the biggest, peered through the window.

"What do you see?" asked the cock.

"There's a table laden with food and drink and there are men counting out lots of money," whispered the donkey.

"Let me see," said the dog, the cat, and the cock.

The dog climbed up onto the donkey's back. The cat jumped onto the dog's back and the cock flew onto the cat's head. That way they could all see through the window.

"Let's sing," suggested the donkey. "Maybe they will then give us some of their supper."

So the donkey brayed, the dog barked, the cat yowled and the cock crowed.

The men, who were really robbers, had never heard such a noise before. They jumped up in panic and ran out of the house, leaving the door wide open.

The four animals went in and enjoyed a good meal from the robbers' table. Then they all went to sleep. The donkey slept in the yard, the dog stretched out behind the door, the cat curled up on the warm hearth, and the cock perched on a beam in the roof.

Some time later, one of the robbers came creeping back to the house. Everything was in darkness when he went in, so he tried to light a candle. As he did so, the cat woke up. The robber saw the cat's yellow eyes shining and thought they were coals glowing on the fire. He held out the match toward them, but what a fright he got! The cat sprang at him, spitting and scratching. The robber ran for the door and tripped over the dog. The dog jumped up and bit his leg. The robber dashed across the yard, waking the donkey, who kicked him hard as he ran past. Finally, the cock flew down, crowing and screeching with all his might.

The terrified robber ran back to the others, crying, "There's a monster in the house. I was scratched, bitten, and kicked, and the screeching and screaming were terrible! We must never go back there again!"

And they never did. The animals liked the robbers' house so much, they lived there together for the rest of their lives.

THE STORY OF SIR GARETH

Long ago, in the days of King Arthur, it was the custom on special feast days for the king to grant a stranger's request. And so it was that on the Feast of Pentecost, a young stranger in humble dress entered the Great Hall at Camelot.

"Sire," said the youth, "all I ask is that you let me eat and drink at your table for a year and then that you grant me two more requests."

A murmur of surprise and scorn ran through the hall.

"Why not ask for something better?" said the king. But the young man shook his head.

"That is all I desire," he said.

"Tell me your name," said the king. But again the young man shook his head.

"I cannot tell you yet, Sire."

The king took a liking to the young man. He turned to Sir Kay, his steward, and asked him to feed the youth and to look after him well. But Sir Kay glanced at the youth without a name and muttered, "He shall work in the kitchen and eat scraps of fat. By the end of the year he'll be as fat as a pig. He has no name, so I will call him Beaumains, or Fairhands."

The young man was angry, but he kept his temper and said nothing. Sir Kay gave him a place at the table by the hall door, among the serving boys.

Beaumains worked, and even slept, in the kitchens like the scullery boys. But he never complained. As the days passed, Beaumains grew taller and stronger, but Sir Kay never let him join the other knights in their practices.

Nevertheless, Beaumains watched the knights jousting whenever he could and learned their every move.

The year passed by and it was Pentecost again. This time, as the king sat at the great feast, a lady came to him with a request. Her name was Lady Linnet and she begged the king to

send one of his knights to help her sister, Lady Leonise, who was held a prisoner in her own castle by the Red Knight.

As the king looked around for one of his knights to send on this quest, Beaumains pushed his way from the far end of the hall to stand before him.

"Sire," he said, "a year has now passed and I ask my two other requests. First, that you send me to help this lady and, second, that when I return, I be made a knight."

"Your requests are granted," smiled the king.

But Lady Linnet was not at all pleased.

"Is this kitchen page the only help you will give me?" she demanded and she stormed out of the castle.

At that moment, to everyone's surprise, a messenger came in to say that Beaumain's horse and armor were ready. Now Beaumain's real name was Gareth and he was the youngest son of the Queen of Orkney. He had come to King Arthur in disguise because he wanted to become a Knight of the Round Table through his own brave deeds rather than through his family name. Gareth put on his armor, mounted his mighty warhorse and galloped away after Lady Linnet. Sir Kay tried to stop him, but Gareth brushed him aside and rode on. Soon, he had caught up with Lady Linnet.

"What are you doing here, serving boy?" she called. "Go back to your kitchen."

But Gareth kept his temper and said nothing.

They rode on for many months and had several adventures. Gradually, Gareth's good manners and bravery won Lady Linnet's affection.

At last, they arrived at the castle of Lady Leonise. She watched from a window as Sir Gareth prepared to fight her captor, the Red Knight.

"Take care," Lady Linnet warned him. "The Red Knight is a cruel and wicked man. He has already killed more than forty brave knights."

As she spoke, the Red Knight galloped up, shouting, "The lady and all her land are mine."

"We'll see about that," replied Sir Gareth, and charged straight at the Red Knight. Both men were thrown from their horses and lay so still on the ground that it was feared their necks were broken. But they quickly sprang to their feet, swords in hand. They hacked and slashed at one another until pieces of armour flew in all directions. Blow upon blow rained upon both helmets. On they fought, but neither would give in. At last,

Gareth knocked the Red Knight to the ground and held him there at his mercy.

"I will spare your life," he said, "if you give up your claim to the Lady Leonise and all her lands."

The Red Knight had to agree and Gareth let him go.

And so it came to pass that, at the end of the year, Gareth was made a full Knight of the Round Table, as he had been promised. He and Lady Linnet were later married and King Arthur himself came to the wedding to give them his blessing.

THE PIED PIPER OF HAMELIN

Long, long ago, the town of Hamelin in Germany was badly troubled by rats. They were everywhere. They ran about in the stores and in the houses. They bit the babies, they fought the dogs, and killed the cats. They slept in the beds and even made their nests inside people's best hats. They ate up all the food in the store cupboards and made such a terrible noise with their shrieking and squeaking that at last the people of Hamelin could stand it no longer. They marched angrily down to the Town Hall and demanded that the mayor do something to get rid of the rats once and for all.

Now the mayor was old and very lazy.

"What can I do?" he cried. "I've thought until my head aches, wondering how to set a trap to catch those rats."

Just as he said this, there was a tap-tapping at the door and in came the strangest man you ever saw. He was tall and thin, with piercing blue eyes and a mocking smile. His clothes were half red and half yellow and on a cord around his neck hung a musical pipe.

The mayor and all the people stared at him.

"Who are you?" asked the mayor.

"They call me the Pied Piper," replied the young man. "I can rid your town of rats. What will you give me in return?"

"A bag of gold," replied the mayor without hesitation.

"Is that a promise?" asked the Piper.

"Yes, yes, of course," snapped the mayor. "I give you my word of honor."

The Piper smiled and stepped out into the street. He put his pipe to his lips and began to play a strange little tune. At first it was soft and slow, then it became high and piercing. It could be heard in every corner of the town. Then, as the people watched and listened, rats of every size, shape, and color, young and old, came rushing and tumbling from every nook and cranny into the streets.

The Piper began to walk slowly through the town and the rats raced along behind him. He led them down to the river, then turned sharply and stepped aside. But all the rats ran on. They plunged down into the water and were drowned, every one, except an old, fat one. She was so fat that she floated and drifted away to Ratland, where she lived to tell her grandchildren of the music that had lured the rats on to an imaginary dreamland of rich food and giant cheeses.

Now that all the rats had gone the Piper went back to the Town Hall. All the people cheered and shouted as he approached the mayor!

"Your rats are gone for ever," he said. "Now I've come for my reward—the bag of gold you promised me."

But the mayor just smiled and said to the people, "Why should we give this stranger so much money? After all, he only piped a tune to lead the rats away."

132

The people all agreed. How quickly they had forgotten the mayor's promise and the wonderful service the Piper had done for them!

The mayor picked up one gold coin from the bag and tossed it to the Piper.

"That should be payment enough," he said.

The Piper's blue eyes flashed with anger. Then he said softly, "I know another tune for those who try to trick me."

"Play what you like," blustered the mayor. "You do not scare us. Do your worst."

Once more the Piper stepped into the street. He put his pipe to his lips and began to play. This time it was a different tune. The music was sweet and wonderfully strange.

Suddenly, all the children of Hamelin came running along the street, tripping, skipping, shouting, laughing. And the strangest thing of all was that, while the music made the children dance and sing, it made all the people of the town stand as still as stone statues. They watched helplessly as their children followed the Piper down to the river.

"Our children will be drowned!" they sobbed.

But the Piper turned away from the river, toward the steep mountain, with the children dancing happily behind him.

"They can't get through the mountain. They'll have to come back now," cried the people of Hamelin.

134

But, just as the Piper reached the mountainside, a door opened. The Piper went through, followed by all the children, except for one—a little lame boy who could not keep up with the others and who did not reach the door before it shut. Sad and lonely without his friends, he returned home. He told his parents what had happened: "The music was leading us toward a happy land where no one was lame and where children played all day long."

The people never saw their children again, for the Piper took them far away from Hamelin. But they named a street in the town "Pied Piper Street" in their memory.

THE FLIPPITYFLAP

There once was a man called Bartek, whose job it was to guard his master's animals against attacks from wolves. Bartek enjoyed his work, but he was not a very good shot with his gun. Usually when he tried to shoot, he missed.

One day, Bartek missed his target at close range.

"I would give anything to be a good shot!" he groaned.

As he said this, a strange man in a tall hat and cloak came toward him through the trees. Bartek pointed his gun at the stranger and demanded to know what he wanted.

"For a small price," replied the stranger, "I will use my magic to make you into a perfect shot."

Bartek liked this idea.

"All I ask," continued the stranger, "is that when I return at the end of one year, you show me a rare bird. If I cannot name it, then the magic power will be yours for always. But, if I name the bird correctly, then you must come and be my slave for ever. What do you say?"

"I agree," cried Bartek happily.

The stranger smiled. Then he took off his hat and, with a mocking gesture, bowed low. As he did so, Bartek saw two horns on top of the stranger's head and a hint of a tail peeping out from beneath his cloak. The stranger was none other than the dreaded Forest Demon!

Bartek aimed his gun at the Demon, fired and missed. The Demon roared with laughter, making the trees shake and the earth quiver. Then he chanted a magic rhyme, twirled around three times and vanished.

"Oh no, what have I done?" moaned the terrified Bartek.

Then he saw a beautiful new gun lying on the grass. It glinted in the sunlight and Bartek saw his name engraved in gold letters on the barrel. He was so excited at finding the gun, he forgot all about the Demon. He picked it up and carried it proudly home.

From that day on, Bartek was a perfect shot and his skill became well known throughout the land. But, as the days passed, he began to worry about his bargain with the Demon.

One sunny morning, as he was eating his breakfast outside his cottage, a woman came toward him. She was quite the ugliest woman Bartek had ever seen.

"I've lost my black and white cow," she said. "I was taking her to market to sell as I have no money left to buy food. Now I shall surely starve."

Bartek felt sorry for the woman.

"Look," he said, "I'm just having breakfast. You can share it, if you like."

"You're very kind," the woman said. Then after eating a bowl of porridge, she exclaimed, "That's the last good meal I shall have, now I've lost my cow."

Bartek then told her of his own troubles.

"I have a marvelous idea," said the woman when he had finished. "I am no beauty, as you can see, but I have a great imagination. I can help you win your bargain with the Demon, but, first, you must marry me."

"What?" spluttered Bartek, falling off his stool in shock.

"I promise you will not be sorry," said the woman. "And I will use my imagination to help you."

So Bartek agreed to marry the ugly woman, thinking that it was better than being a slave to the Demon for ever.

After they were married, Bartek was pleasantly surprised. He and his wife got on very well; they enjoyed each other's company and Bartek soon grew to love his ugly wife. But one thing troubled him. She had not once mentioned how she would save him from the Demon. Had she tricked him, he wondered sadly?

On the very day the Demon was due to return, Bartek's wife began behaving very strangely. She took a pillow from the bed, unpicked the seams and shook all the feathers out on to the floor. Next she went to a large barrel of honey. Bartek watched in amazement as she climbed inside. Then she stepped out again, dripping with honey, and rolled over and over in the feathers until she was completely covered. She was no longer an ugly woman but a very strange bird!

"Dearest husband," she said, "you see before you a rare bird called a flippityflap. Remember that when the Demon comes. I am a flippityflap."

Very soon, a voice called from outside, "Bartek! I have come for you!"

It was the Demon on the rooftop.

"Not so fast," replied Bartek. "First, you must tell me the name of my rare bird."

"Yes, yes," snapped the demon impatiently. "Bring it out."

Bartek opened the door and out hopped the strangest bird the Demon had ever seen. It squawked and flapped about while the puzzled Demon scratched his head. At last he said, "I've never seen such a bird before. It can't be real."

"Not real?" replied Bartek. "Take care, sir, what you say. A flippityflap is easily offended and vicious when it attacks."

"A flippityflap," snarled the Demon.

The flippityflap advanced menacingly toward the Demon. He was terrified and leaped into the air, lashing and thrashing his tail. Then he ran off into the forest and was never seen or heard of again.

A very relieved Bartek helped his wife wash off her feathers and in no time at all she was her own ugly self again.

The next day, as they were having breakfast, a black and white cow appeared at their door.

"This just goes to show," said Bartek contentedly, "what a lucky man I am. Now I have a black and white cow, a first-rate gun, and the most wonderful wife in the world."

THUMBELINA

There was once a woman who longed to have a child. One day, she decided to go to an old witch and ask her for help. The witch gave her a small seed and told her to plant it in the ground. The woman thanked her and went home.

Now the seed was a magic seed and no sooner had the woman planted it than it began to grow into a beautiful flower, rather like a tulip, with tightly closed petals.

"How lovely!" said the woman when she saw the flower. She kissed it and the most wonderful thing happened. The flower opened up and there, right in the middle of it, was a tiny girl no bigger than the woman's thumb.

The woman was overjoyed.

"I'll call her Thumbelina," she said to herself.

At night, Thumbelina slept in a bed made from a polished walnut shell. She had violet petals for her mattress and a rose petal for her quilt. During the day, she played on a table near the window. The woman put a bowl of water there with a large petal floating on it. Thumbelina used the petal as a boat and had two white horsehairs for oars. She was very happy and would sing softly to herself as she rowed up and down.

One night, while Thumbelina was fast asleep, an ugly toad hopped in through the open window. When he saw Thumbelina, he thought how pretty she was. He took the walnut shell, with Thumbelina asleep inside, and carried it away to the river where he lived. There he put Thumbelina down upon a water lily leaf that floated in the middle of the river.

When Thumbelina woke up and looked around her, she did not know where she was. Then she saw the toad.

"You are to be my wife," said the toad. "I am going down into the mud now to get our home ready." And he dived down into the water.

Thumbelina cried and cried. She did not want to marry the big ugly toad and live in the mud.

The little fishes in the river felt very sorry for Thumbelina, so they nibbled through the stem of the lily leaf until it broke away from the plant. The lily leaf drifted downstream, taking Thumbelina far away from the ugly toad. At last, it was caught in the rushes on the river bank and came to a stop. Thumbelina climbed off, glad to be on dry land once more.

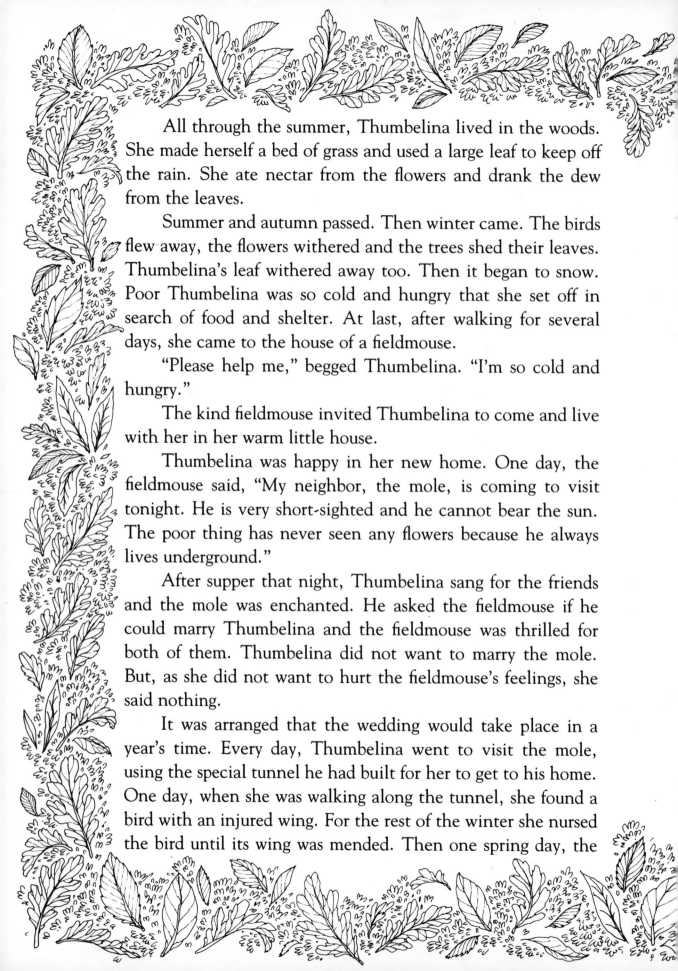

All through the summer, Thumbelina lived in the woods. She made herself a bed of grass and used a large leaf to keep off the rain. She ate nectar from the flowers and drank the dew from the leaves.

Summer and autumn passed. Then winter came. The birds flew away, the flowers withered and the trees shed their leaves. Thumbelina's leaf withered away too. Then it began to snow. Poor Thumbelina was so cold and hungry that she set off in search of food and shelter. At last, after walking for several days, she came to the house of a fieldmouse.

"Please help me," begged Thumbelina. "I'm so cold and hungry."

The kind fieldmouse invited Thumbelina to come and live with her in her warm little house.

Thumbelina was happy in her new home. One day, the fieldmouse said, "My neighbor, the mole, is coming to visit tonight. He is very short-sighted and he cannot bear the sun. The poor thing has never seen any flowers because he always lives underground."

After supper that night, Thumbelina sang for the friends and the mole was enchanted. He asked the fieldmouse if he could marry Thumbelina and the fieldmouse was thrilled for both of them. Thumbelina did not want to marry the mole. But, as she did not want to hurt the fieldmouse's feelings, she said nothing.

It was arranged that the wedding would take place in a year's time. Every day, Thumbelina went to visit the mole, using the special tunnel he had built for her to get to his home. One day, when she was walking along the tunnel, she found a bird with an injured wing. For the rest of the winter she nursed the bird until its wing was mended. Then one spring day, the bird was strong enough to leave. As it flew up into the sunlight, it called, "Thank you for saving my life, Thumbelina. I won't forget you."

The day of the wedding finally arrived. Thumbelina was very unhappy. She did not love the mole and she hated the thought of living deep underground. She crept out of the fieldmouse's home to look at the sunlight for the last time and, as she gazed up at the clear sky, she saw a bird flying toward her. It was the bird whose life she had saved.

"I told you I would not forget you," called the bird. "Come with me and I will take you to a wonderful land."

Thumbelina quickly climbed onto the bird's back and away he flew, over the mountains to a land where the sun always shone and flowers and fruit grew everywhere.

145

The bird put Thumbelina down upon the most beautiful white flower. It was as clear and bright as polished glass and inside was a little man no bigger than Thumbelina. He was the King of the Flower People and, as soon as he saw Thumbelina, he fell in love with her. He asked her to be his wife and queen of all the flowers and Thumbelina happily agreed. Then, from each flower, came a tiny person with a present for her. Best of all was a pair of wings to fasten on her back so that she could fly from flower to flower.

When the wedding was over, the little bird had to leave. He flew far away to the country of Denmark. There he made a nest just above the window of a man who wrote fairy stories. He sang to the man every day and told him some of his own stories. That is how the man came to know the story of Thumbelina. He wrote it down and now you have heard the story too.

The Walrus and The Carpenter

The sun was shining on the sea,
Shining with all his might:
He did his very best to make
The billows smooth and bright—
And this was odd, because it was
The middle of the night.

The moon was shining sulkily,
Because she thought the sun
Had got no business to be there
After the day was done—
"It's very rude of him," she said,
"To come and spoil the fun."

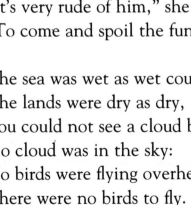

The sea was wet as wet could be,
The lands were dry as dry,
You could not see a cloud because
No cloud was in the sky:
No birds were flying overhead—
There were no birds to fly.

The Walrus and the Carpenter
Were walking close at hand;
They wept like anything to see
Such quantities of sand:
"If this were only cleared away."
They said, "it *would* be grand."

"If seven maids with seven mops
Swept it for half a year,
Do you suppose," the Walrus said,
"That they could get it clear?"
"I doubt it," said the Carpenter,
And shed a bitter tear.

"O Oysters, come and walk with us,"
The Walrus did beseech.
"A pleasant walk, a pleasant talk,
Along the briny beach:
We cannot do with more than four,
To give a hand to each."

The eldest Oyster looked at him,
But never a word he said:
The eldest Oyster winked his eye,
And shook his heavy head—
Meaning to say he did not choose
To leave the oyster bed.

But four young oysters hurried up,
All eager for the treat;
Their coats were brushed, their faces washed,
Their shoes were clean and neat—
And this was odd, because, you know,
They hadn't any feet.

Four other oysters followed them,
And yet another four;
And thick and fast they came at last,
And more, and more, and more—
All hopping through the sandy waves,
And scrambling to the shore.

The Walrus and the Carpenter
Walked out a mile or so,
And then they rested on a rock
Conveniently low.
And all the little Oysters stood
And waited in a row.

"The time has come," the Walrus said,
"To talk of many things:
Of shoes—and ships—and sealing wax—
Of cabbages—and kings—
And why the sea is boiling hot—
And whether pigs have wings."

"But wait a bit," the Oysters cried,
"Before we have our chat;
For some of us are out of breath,
And all of us are fat!"
"No hurry!" said the Carpenter.
They thanked him much for that.

"A loaf of bread," the Walrus said,
"Is what we chiefly need:
Pepper and vinegar besides,
Are very good indeed—
Now if you're ready, Oysters dear,
We can begin to feed."

"But not on us!" the Oysters cried,
Turning a little blue.
"After such kindness, that would be
A dismal thing to do!"
"The night is fine," the Walrus said.
"Do you admire the view?"

"It was so kind of you to come!
And you are very nice!"
The Carpenter said nothing but
"Cut us another slice:
I wish you were not quite so deaf—
I've had to ask you twice!"

"It seems a shame," the Walrus said,
"To play them such a trick,
After we've brought them out so far,
And made them trot so quick!"
The Carpenter said nothing but
"The butter's spread too thick."

"I weep for you," the Walrus said:
"I deeply sympathize."
With sobs and tears he sorted out
Those of the largest size,
Holding his pocket handkerchief
Before his streaming eyes.

"O Oysters," said the Carpenter,
"You've had a pleasant run!
Shall we be trotting home again?"
But answer came there none—
And this was scarcely odd, because
They'd eaten every one.

RED UMBRELLA
AND
YELLOW SCARF

Monkey put on his yellow scarf.

"It is warm today," said Marmoset. "That yellow scarf is useless, Monkey."

Monkey opened his red umbrella and held it high above his head.

"It is dry today," said Marmoset. "That red umbrella is useless, Monkey."

Monkey did not say a word. He smiled, and walked away through the jungle, his yellow scarf around his neck, his red umbrella above his head.

He came to a stream and saw Jacana. Jacana Bird stepped along on the bank, and her five little chicks bobbed and scuttled behind her, black and golden, like bumble bees.

Mother Jacana turned her head, fluttering yellow wings at the chicks.

"Now we must cross the stream," she said. "You are far too fluffy and small for swimming. Here is a pathway of lily pad leaves. Walk carefully, chicks. The water is deep."

The shiny round leaves lay still on the water, making a pathway from bank to bank. Jacana stepped on a lily pad, spreading out her long, thin toes.

"Come," she called. "This leaf is safe."

The five little chicks hopped on the leaf, and cheeped as it dipped and swayed beneath them.

Mother Jacana stepped to the next leaf.

"Come," she called. "*This* leaf is safe." And the five little chicks scuttled behind her.

Now they were halfway across the stream.

"Come," called Mother Jacana again.

Four little chicks scuttled behind her. The last one stood still, looking at a lily bud.

"Why have you closed yourself up?" he asked. "What are you hiding inside you, lily bud?"

He pushed his beak between the petals and wriggled his head inside the bud. And he found himself staring into the eyes of the biggest brown bee he had ever seen.

"Buzz!" went the bee. The chick fell backward and slid across the lily pad, splashing in the stream among the little silver bubbles.

Monkey did not have a boat. But he had his scarf, and he had his umbrella. He turned the umbrella upside down, so that it floated on the water. He tied on the yellow scarf for a sail. Then he sat in his red umbrella-boat, and sailed down the stream to Jacana chick. He lifted him gently out of the water, and set him down on the lily pad. Jacana chick jumped up and down on the leaf, shaking the water out of his fluff. Then he bobbed and scuttled after his mother. When mother Jacana turned around, there were five little chicks on the leaf behind her.

"Come," she said. "We have reached the bank."

Monkey walked away from the stream, his yellow scarf around his neck, his red umbrella above his head. He came to a cliff, and sat down to rest. He heard a little snuffling sound, and leaned out over the cliff to look. A soft, round, golden-brown creature was clinging to a creeper rope. She lifted her small furry face to Monkey, staring with unhappy eyes.

"Be careful, Little Opossum," called Monkey. "Don't fall onto those rocks below."

Little Opossum started to climb, clinging tightly with her claws, moving up and up the creeper until she was close to the top of the cliff. Monkey stretched out a paw to help her.

Snap! The creeper broke in half!

"Oh-ee-ee!" cried Little Opossum. Down she fell to the rocks below.

Monkey did not have a ladder. But he had his scarf, and he had his umbrella. He turned the umbrella upside down and tied it to the yellow scarf. Then he lay on the grass at the edge of the cliff and gently lowered the red umbrella until it rested by Little Opossum.

Little Opossum sat in the umbrella. It rocked as Monkey pulled it up, and Little Opossum hid her face in her paws.

"You are safe," said Monkey. "Open your eyes."

Little Opossum climbed from the umbrella, and trotted happily over the grass.

Monkey walked away from the cliff, his yellow scarf around his neck, his red umbrella above his head. He went to the mud flats and sat on a shell bank. He shaded his eyes from the sun with his paw, and looked across at the mangrove trees standing on tangled roots in the mud. Among the roots sat angry red crabs, guarding the doors of their tunnel homes. The crabs that sat in the branches above were thin and gray, with bright red claws. They stared at the screeching yellow parrots busily flying from tree to tree.

Then Monkey saw Turtle. Poor old Turtle was trying to find his way to the shell bank. He was old and tired, and he seemed to be lost as he plodded along by the mangrove trees.

"Keep away, keep away!" called the angry red crabs.

"Get out, get out!" screamed the thin gray crabs.

"Chase him away!" screeched the yellow parrots.

Turtle did not know where to turn.

"This way, Turtle," Monkey called.

Turtle turned toward the shell bank. The angry red crabs, the thin gray crabs, and the screeching parrots pinched him and bit him, and chased him over the mud to the shell bank. There they turned him on his back, and left him in the hot sun.

"Poor old Turtle," Monkey said. He put out a paw and lifted old Turtle, setting him gently on to his legs. But Turtle could not move away. The sun was too hot, and his feet were too sore. He wanted to sleep until he felt better.

Monkey did not have a bed. But he had his scarf, and he had his umbrella.

He folded the scarf to make a bed, and stood the umbrella

beside it, for shade. Then he lifted poor old Turtle again, and put him down on the yellow bed. Turtle sighed, and closed his eyes.

When the sun went down behind the mangroves, Turtle smiled, and stretched his legs. Then he stumped away happily home to his supper.

"And I must go home to *my* supper," said Monkey.

He smiled to himself as he walked away, his yellow scarf around his neck, his red umbrella above his head.

As soon as he reached his tree in the jungle, he took off his scarf and folded it neatly.

"It was warm today," said Marmoset. "That yellow scarf was useless, Monkey."

Monkey closed the red umbrella and hung it carefully over a branch.

"It was dry today," said Marmoset. "That red umbrella was useless, Monkey."

Monkey did not say a word. Later, perhaps, he would tell Marmoset. But now it was time for his supper.